THE REAL US

TOMMY GREENWALD

THE REAL US

ILLUSTRATED BY J.P. COOVERT

Roaring Brook Press · New York

Text copyright © 2017 by Tommy Greenwald
Illustrations copyright © 2017 by J.P. Coovert
Published by Roaring Brook Press
Roaring Brook Press is a division of Holtzbrinck Publishing Holdings
Limited Partnership
175 Fifth Avenue, New York, NY 10010
mackids.com

Library of Congress Cataloging-in-Publication Data

Names: Greenwald, Tom, 1962– author. | Coovert, J. P., illustrator.
Title: The real us / Tommy Greenwald ; illustrated by J.P. Coovert.
Description: First edition. | New York : Roaring Brook Press, 2017. |
    Summary: Told from different viewpoints, everything changes when Calista
    Getz, always known as the prettiest girl in school, gets a pimple shortly
    before the big eighth-grade dance.
Identifiers: LCCN 2016039883 (print) | LCCN 2017011426 (ebook) | ISBN
    9781626721715 (hardback) | ISBN 9781626721722 (Ebook)
Subjects: | CYAC: Beauty, Personal—Fiction. | Friendship—Fiction. | Middle
    schools—Fiction. | Schools—Fiction. | Humorous stories. | BISAC:
    JUVENILE FICTION / Humorous Stories. | JUVENILE FICTION /
    Social Issues / Friendship.
Classification: LCC PZ7.G8523 Re 2017 (print) | LCC PZ7.G8523 (ebook) | DDC
    [Fic]—dc23
LC record available at https://lccn.loc.gov/2016039883

Our books may be purchased in bulk for promotional, educational, or business use.
Please contact your local bookseller or the Macmillan Corporate and Premium Sales
Department at (800) 221-7945 ext. 5442 or by e-mail at MacmillanSpecialMarkets@
macmillan.com.

First edition 2017
Printed in the United States of America by LSC Communications, Harrisonburg, Virginia

10 9 8 7 6 5 4 3 2 1

To Fred Klompston

"Imperfection is beauty."
—Marilyn Monroe

PROLOGUE

She was always the prettiest girl in the room.

When she was little, her parents used to show her off to adults. Then they'd pretend to be surprised when the compliments started pouring in.

"Oh, isn't she the cutest little thing!"

"Look at her in that dress! What an absolute doll!"

"You two are going to have your hands full when she gets older; she's going to drive all the boys crazy!"

"Oh, come on, you're just being nice," her parents would say, but they knew.

And soon enough, she *knew.*

By the time she was in elementary school, she could tell that people were treating her as if she were special. Girls wanted to be her best friend. Boys stared at her from a distance. Even teachers were extra nice. It took a little while, but she got used to it.

Then she started liking it.

Then she started needing it.

And before long, it became who she was. It didn't matter that she liked reading, or was the high scorer on the soccer team, or took dance classes. She was Calista Getz, the pretty girl. The prettiest girl in the room. The most beautiful girl in the whole school!

Until she wasn't.

MONDAY

CALISTA

"AAAAAGGHHHGHGHGHGHGHHH!"

I yell like a lunatic when I see my best friends in the whole world, Ellie and Ella, running toward me.

"AAAAAIIIIEEEEEEEEE!" they scream back. We hug for about five minutes. We talk at each other for five more minutes, but none of us can hear a word anyone else is saying. People are staring, but we don't care. We're back together again, and it's great.

Then the bell rings, and the school year begins.

DAMIAN

I don't like it when girls yell at the top of their lungs. It's really distracting and annoying.

So when I see three girls acting crazy, like one of them just got back from a war or something, I walk by them as fast as I can and go into the classroom.

It's not until I'm sitting down that I realize one of them is Calista Getz.

CALISTA

We take our seats in first period, and I notice that two of the fluorescent light bulbs in the ceiling are flickering. Seriously? On the first day of school? No wonder the teachers are always complaining about budget cuts.

"I can't believe you're sitting next to Patrick Toole," Ellie whispers from two rows away.

"Sssssshhhhh!" I say. Ellie looks wounded, so I add, "Oh, don't be so sensitive." People take everything I say and do so seriously. It's kind of ridiculous.

I glance over to my right. "Hey, Patrick."

Patrick smiles, and his white teeth practically blind me. Okay, not really, but his teeth are extremely white. Also, you could probably build a swimming pool in one of his dimples.

"Did you have a good summer?" he asks.

"It was okay, I guess." Rule number one: Never sound too excited in front of a guy.

"Cool." Patrick looks down. He's shy in front of me. Everyone is shy in front of me, except the obnoxious boys—like Patrick's friend Will Hanson, whose only goal in life is to show off in front of his friends.

"Looking super hot, Calista!" Will says, right on cue. "Like, solar system hot!"

I try to laugh, just to be nice. I do that a lot—try to make boys feel better by laughing at their jokes. The truth is, I'm a nice person, but because I'm pretty, people don't always believe it.

"Shut up, Will," Patrick says, then turns back to me. "I'm glad you had an okay summer."

"How was yours?"

"Good, thanks."

Patrick is the me of boys. He's really cute. Everyone always thinks we should become boyfriend and girlfriend, even though I barely know him. People don't care about that, though. They just think the two most good-looking kids in the grade should go out. I guess that makes sense.

"Let's get started," says our teacher, Ms. Harnick, and my conversation with Patrick is over.

For now.

DAMIAN

"Damian White," calls Ms. Harnick.

I raise my hand. "Here."

She nods. "Welcome, Mr. White."

I put my hand down quickly. I don't like to raise my hand.

"Hey! Damian!"

I look over to my left. Will Hanson is leaning over his desk, in my direction. He has red hair and braces, and he's smiling, but not out of friendliness.

"What?"

"How was your summer?"

"It was fine."

"The weather was pretty brutal this year. So humid. That must've been tough."

I don't answer him. I feel my skin start to get sticky.

Will keeps needling me. "Do you ever take that red jacket off, by the way? What are you hiding?"

"I'm not hiding anything."

"Leave him alone," says a girl sitting behind us. I can't remember her name. She smiles at me.

Will turns around. "Hey, Laura, why don't you mind your own business? Go grab a burger or something."

The girl's eyes flash. "Real original, Will."

Will turn backs to me. "Now, where were we?"

My whole back is wet.

It's a good thing I have extra shirts in my locker.

LAURA

Will Hanson is a jerk. As if I would ever let anyone like him get to me!

That's what I tell myself, anyway.

As soon as class is dismissed, the kid Will was making fun of hurries to the door. He was new last year, but I recognize him right away. He's really tall, and he always wears the same red jacket, even if it's really hot out.

As he passes my desk, he notices me and hesitates for just a second.

"Thanks," he says. "For before."

"No problem," I say, but he's gone so fast he doesn't hear me.

CALISTA

After first period, everyone rushes out into the hall-way. Ellie and Ella surround me as we walk to our next class. They're basically blocking me off from everyone else, because they want me for themselves.

"So, have you decided?" Ellie asks.

Ella nods eagerly. "Yeah, have you made up your mind?" The general rule is that Ellie talks first, then Ella says the same thing, but slightly differently.

I shrug, pretending not to know what they're talking about. "Decided what?"

Ellie and Ella stare at each other as if they're having an eye-widening contest.

"The dance!" they both blurt out at once.

"Who are you going with?" Ellie asks.

"To the dance!" Ella adds, as if I'd forgotten what they said one second earlier. "Everyone wants to know!"

"I haven't really thought about it, if you want to know the truth," I say, which isn't technically the truth.

Ellie leans in even closer. "What about Patrick?"

"What about him?"

"You know!" squeals Ella, and they both dissolve into a fit of giggles. I shrug, throw in a little eye roll, and notice Laura Corbett walking slightly behind us. Laura was my best friend in elementary school. We're still friends, but it's different now.

"Laurasaurus," I say. "What's up?"

Ella and Ellie immediately stop laughing and turn their attention to the intruder.

"What do you want?" Ellie sneers.

"Yeah, do you need something?" Ella chimes in.

I smile at Laura in what I hope is a friendly way.

She tries to smile back.

LAURA

"Why so serious, Ellie?" I say. "Or is it Ella? I always get you guys mixed up."

"You are so not funny," Ellie says. "Go away."

"Yeah, scram," echoes Ella.

I throw up my hands. "Come on! The school year just began. Can't we all just be friends?"

"Har dee har HAR," Ellie sneers.

"Oooh, how clever," I sneer back. Calista looks like she's already bored with this idiotic exchange. Not that I blame her.

"What's up?" she says.

I stare at Calista, still trying to understand why my former best friend hangs around with these girls.

"Uh, hey Callie. I'm just making sure you're coming to practice later?"

She smiles, and for a second I see the girl that used to kick the ball with me for hours and hours in the yard behind my house. We used to call each other "besties for life." That seems like a pretty long time ago.

"No one calls her 'Callie' anymore," Ella announces. "And Calista can't talk to you right now. We're talking about the dance."

"Oooh, don't let me stop you," I say. This Friday night we have the First Week Dance, where all the eighth graders (who have gone to school together pretty much all their lives) get reacquainted in a big dark room, with the floor sticky from fruit punch and loud pounding music that occasionally gets people to jump up and down with their arms in the air. It's fun for twenty minutes and kind of annoying the rest of the time. And it's fun for the cool kids and kind of annoying for the rest of us.

But it's all anyone wants to talk about.

"Callie?" I say, trying to get my answer. "Are you coming later or not?"

"To soccer practice?" Ellie asks, wrinkling her nose like she just smelled a dead squirrel. She twists her head toward Calista. "Tell me you're not playing soccer this year!"

We all wait. This is an important answer—for Ellie, Ella, and myself, anyway. Calista looks like she really couldn't care less.

"I guess so," she says, finally. "My parents would be, like, so mad if I quit." I pray that no one notices my huge sigh of relief. Calista smiles at me. "See you later, Laurasaurus?"

Laurasaurus is her nickname for me, from the old days. I really liked it back then. Now I'm not so sure. It makes me sound—let's see, how should I put this—huge.

"Yep, definitely." I start to walk away, since my work here is done. But Ellie has one last question for me.

"Do you play goalie?" she asks. "Because you kind of look like you could totally block the goal all by yourself."

Ellie and Ella dissolve into hysterics. I look at Calista, who doesn't seem amused. But she doesn't seem mad, either. She doesn't seem anything.

"No, I don't play goalie," I answer. "I play defense. And you better watch it before I defense your butt with my foot."

That shuts them up.

I walk away.

CALISTA

I feel bad when I see Laura leave. I want to say something, but I don't. I can't. I don't know why I can't, but I just can't.

"I can't believe you two used to be friends," Ellie says.

I stare at Ellie.

"We still are," I say.

DAMIAN

I wish they had assigned seats at lunch. It would make life a lot easier.

But they don't, so I sit with Jeffrey Klantz. We started eating lunch together halfway through last year. I take out the same thing I eat every day: a peanut butter and apple sandwich.

I also take out my notebook and start sketching.

"What are you drawing?" Jeffrey asks. "Wait, let me guess: A desert."

Everyone who knows me knows I like to draw deserts. Hilly, sandy, hot, dry deserts. I don't know why. I've just always done it.

"Yes," I say.

Jeffrey pulls out his lunch bag and starts eating. I keep drawing, pausing every once in a while to take a bite of my sandwich. Jeffrey and I don't talk to each other very much. But I like that he's there.

"Look," Jeffrey says, suddenly.

I look up. He's pointing across the cafeteria. There's some sort of fuss going on at the table closest to the door. That's the table where Calista sits.

Calista Getz.

I think about Calista a lot. Everyone thinks about Calista a lot, probably. But I bet I think about her more. She was the first girl I met when I moved to Easton last year. She showed me around the school, and she was very friendly. I remember when she pointed out where the nurse's office was, she said, "Hopefully you won't have to spend too much time in here." I said, "I hope so, too." She smiled her nice smile, waved, and walked away.

That was the last real conversation we ever had.

CALISTA

"Leave me out of it," I say, sitting in my usual seat at the head of the table.

Ellie takes a bite of her salad. "Patrick's shy! He's like perfect-looking, but he's shy!"

"If he wants to ask me, he'll ask me," I say. "If not, I'll live. There are plenty of other fish in the sea."

Ella frowns. "What does that even mean?"

I roll my eyes. "It means if I don't go with Patrick, I'll go with someone else."

The rest of the girls at the table nod their heads like I've just said something incredibly wise. There's Beth, and Camille, and Ginger, and Leslie. Camille is the only one who sometimes actually says what she thinks, even if it means disagreeing with me. I like her, but if I became good friends with her, Ellie and Ella would totally freak out.

"He's looking over here!" Ellie says, elbowing me in

the ribs. "He's smiling! No wait! He's getting up! He's getting up and he's smiling! Let's go talk to him!"

"Let's go what?" I say, but I'm too late. Ellie and Ella suddenly shoot out of their chairs, hurry over to Patrick's table, have an incredibly urgent, eight-second conversation with him, and scamper back.

"Stop being so crazy, you guys," I mumble into my straw. "I mean it."

Ellie looks slightly crushed, the way she always does when I get mad at her. "Sor-RY."

"It's okay," I tell her. She doesn't get it. The whole point with boys is to not let them know you care. You lose control that way.

Ellie quickly recovers. "Well, we probably shouldn't even tell you this since you're being so bossy," she gasps, "but Patrick is going to ask you to the dance tomorrow!"

Ella nods like an out-of-control bobblehead. "He's going to pop the question at lunch! He just told us!"

Without meaning to, I smile. "Really?"

"Really!" they both yell, practically hyperventilating.

"That's nice," I say. Luckily for me, no one can hear my heart pounding.

Camille catches my eye. "Are you relieved?" she asks.

Ellie and Ella laugh.

"Are you serious, Camille?" says Ellie. "As IF!"

"Patrick is the one that should be relieved!" Ella chimes in.

"Well, you never know," Camille says, staring back down at her plate.

She's totally right, of course.

You never know.

"We need to talk about dresses!" says Ellie. "We should plan a trip to the mall!"

"My mom's taking me tomorrow," I say. Ellie and Ella look disappointed, but only for a moment. As everyone starts yammering about what to wear, I sigh and look around, suddenly bored. The first kid I see is Damian White, that really tall kid who always wears a goofy red jacket. He's sitting all the way across the cafeteria with some kid I don't know. The only reason I know who Damian is is because he stood in line in front of me last year when we got our books on the first day of school, and one of the teachers asked me to show him around. He was new. He seemed like an okay kid, maybe a little weird. I heard somewhere that he's a really good artist.

I smile at Damian, but he doesn't smile back.

It's possible he doesn't remember who I am, but I doubt it.

DAMIAN

When Calista lifts her head and stares right at me, I freeze, and my breathing stops.

When she smiles, I quickly stare back down at my plate, then wipe my forehead, which feels a little damp.

"I bet they're talking about the First Week Dance," Jeffrey says.

I wait to speak until my breathing returns to normal. "I suppose so," I say.

"Who do you think she wants to go with?"

"That's none of our business."

Jeffrey laughs. "In this school, everything is everyone's business."

I nod. "Yeah, I guess so."

After a few more deep breaths, I go back to drawing. Jeffrey goes back to eating.

LAURA

At soccer practice, I warm up with my friend Rachel Samuels, who's the goalie.

"You told Will Hanson off?" she says. "I love it!"

"Yeah, it felt good," I admit.

"Who was the kid Will was hassling?"

"I forget his name. The kid who always wears a red jacket; he was new last year."

Rachel nods. "Oh yeah, I know who you're talking about. He's like, super awkward, right?"

"I guess," I say, shrugging. "He seems really sweet."

"All awkward boys are sweet," Rachel says. "Just like all chunky girls."

"Hold on a second!" I tell her. "I'm not sweet."

"And I'm like the opposite of sweet," she says. "I'm like, sooooo sour."

We both crack up.

Coach Sweeney blows the whistle at exactly 4:01.

"Okay, bring it in!" She eyes us over her clipboard. "And no yakking!"

It's the first soccer practice of the year, but we all already know each other, because it's pretty much the same exact team as last spring. Our travel team has been together for three years, and we're almost like sisters at this point. Coach has her work cut out for her if she wants to get our attention.

"Lips equals laps!" she hollers.

We look at her like, huh?

"Anyone who moves their lips gets five laps!"

Aha. That does it. We get real quiet, real fast.

"Guys, this is a big year for Easton Girls Travel," Coach explains. "We're stepping up to the intermediate division, so the competition is going to get a lot tougher. We're going to have to work extra hard. We need to have each other's backs, every practice, every game. We're going to have to—"

She stops suddenly, and scans the field with her eyes. "Where's Calista?"

We all look around, then at each other. Girls start murmuring. Suddenly Jen Costello points up the hill. "There she is!" Everyone turns to see Calista running down the hill, her ponytail swinging back and forth like, well, the tail on a pony, if the pony had gorgeous red hair.

"You're late!" barks Coach Sweeney.

Calista is huffing and puffing. "I know! I'm really sorry!"

"Don't let it happen again, or you'll be in for it!" I sneak a glance at Rachel, and we both roll our eyes. The truth is, Calista will never be in for it from the Coach. She's Coach's favorite. Because she's Calista, and because she's a great player. Sometimes that's just the way it is.

Practice is really intense, and we all work up a real sweat. I end up covering Calista in our scrimmage, which is a good match-up, since she's the best offensive player on the team, and I'm a really good defender. (If you think I just bragged, well, you'd be correct. Sorry folks, but it's true—I rock at defense.)

"Five more minutes!" yells Coach Sweeney. "Next goal wins!"

Calista looks at me. "Let's do this," she says.

"Let's," I say back to her.

It's something we've said to each other before every game for three years.

The next thing I know, Calista has the ball. She dribbles to the sideline, while I try to keep up with her. It's not easy, because she's a little faster than me. (Okay, fine—a lot faster.) I just need to make sure she doesn't slip away.

She makes her move. I follow, right on her heels, sure she's going to sprint all the way to the goal. But she doesn't. She stops suddenly, but I can't stop, and I go flying into her, and all of sudden we're both on the ground, and she's moaning and holding her knee.

My first thought is, *I've injured our best player.*

My second thought is, *Anybody got a hole I can crawl into?*

CALISTA

After about a minute, my knee starts to feel a little better. I scrape the grass off my elbows, check my headband, and slowly get to my feet. I look down at Laura, who's still on the ground, staring up at me with a horrified look on her face.

My first instinct is to try and make her feel better. "I'm fine!" I tell her. "I'm not injured. I'm fine. I thought my knee might have been hurt, but it's not."

"Oh, thank God," she says, panting. "I'm really sorry."

"For what? You were just playing hard."

I wipe my nose and face with my headband, before I realize the headband is too sweaty and gross to do any good. I check my cleats and start heading back to my position, just as Coach Sweeney runs up to me and grabs my shoulders.

"Calista! Calista! Are you okay?" She looks as worried as a mother would be about a daughter.

"Yup, I'm fine. Laura made a good sliding tackle."

Coach looks down at Laura as if noticing her for the first time. "Laura, you have to be more careful. This is a light scrimmage, and you're a big girl. We're all on the same team, remember?"

"We're on the same team?" Laura asks. "Now you tell me! That must be why we're all wearing the same uniforms!"

I hear Rachel, the goalie, giggle quietly—but she's the only one.

"This is no time to be funny, Laura," Coach Sweeney says. "Calista could have been seriously hurt."

"Sorry, Coach," Laura says. "My bad."

Coach blows her whistle. "Game on! Remember, next goal wins!"

As we head back to position, I walk over to Laura. "Hey, she can just be a little uptight sometimes, you know?"

Laura shrugs. "There's no laughter in soccer," she says. "I keep forgetting that." Then she stares at my face. "You have something on your nose."

"I do?" I wipe at my nose, but don't feel anything. "You mean like, a cut?"

She shakes her head. "I guess it's nothing," she says.

A minute later, I score, and practice is over.

DAMIAN

My mom says I started drawing deserts when I was five years old. I don't remember. She's probably right. All I know is that my closet has a lot of drawings in it, and they're all of deserts, and they go back a pretty long time, and I've gotten good at drawing.

After school, I go home, change my shirt, eat some cereal, take my dog, Arfur, for a walk, come back, and draw another desert. This time, I start with the cactus.

The whole time, I'm thinking about Calista smiling at me.

I wish I'm not, but I am.

It's annoying, how your brain works.

You shouldn't have to think about something if you don't want to.

CALISTA

"How was practice?" my mom asks, at dinner.

"Fine," I say.

"Are you excited about the season?"

"I guess."

"Good!" My mom was a great athlete in high school and college, and she's still in amazing shape. She runs every morning. My dad isn't into sports at all. I guess it's kind of the opposite of most families.

"Have you thought about how you're going to balance soccer and dance?" my dad asks. "It's a lot, especially this year, when you really need to do well in school."

"I'll figure it out," I say. I love my parents, except when they're both asking me questions at the same time.

"May I be excused?" asks my little brother, Corey. He likes to hit the Xbox as soon as he finishes shoveling down his food, while the rest of us stay at the table, talking like actual human beings. But tonight, I decide he's on to something.

"Me, too?" I add.

They look at each other, then my mom nods. "Sure, you two—go ahead."

I run up to my room and grab my phone. I text Ellie and Ella for twenty minutes about nothing. Before bed I go to the bathroom to brush my teeth, and as usual I end up looking at my face in the mirror for a while. I look from every angle. I imagine myself with blonde hair. I imagine myself with short hair. I imagine myself with curly hair. I imagine myself with freckles, with blue eyes, with smaller ears.

I like to imagine myself looking all sorts of different ways.

But I know I will never change a thing.

TUESDAY

CALISTA

For some reason, the first thing I think about when I wake up is that kid Damian, and how nervous he looked when I smiled at him in the cafeteria. Maybe I'll try to say hi to him today.

Then I think about Patrick Toole, and my stomach does a somersault.

I immediately reach for my phone to see if anyone has texted me while I was sleeping, and see one from Ellie: TODAY'S THE DAY! Ellie and Ella are eager for Patrick and I to announce we're going to go to the First Week Dance together, because then they can start to figure out whom they're going with, too.

I drag myself out of bed—the worst part of any day, by far—and head to the bathroom. The door is locked. I start pounding.

"Corey! Corey, get out now!"

"In a minute!"

Corey and I get along pretty well, except when we get on each other's nerves, which is most of the time.

I wait ten more seconds, then pound again. "Now, or I'm calling Mom!"

The door flings open. "Fine!" he hisses, marching past me.

I go into the bathroom and splash water on my face. After rubbing my skin with a washcloth, I look in the mirror.

And that's when I see it.

At first, I don't know what it is. I don't recognize it. It doesn't seem possible. But then I lean in for a closer look. My face is practically pressed against the mirror. A sickening feeling starts to spread through my body.

A pimple.

I hear a sound come out of my mouth that I've never heard before: It's like a half groan, half moan, half sigh, half terrified scream. I know that's four halves, but you get what I mean. It wasn't a pretty sound, but apparently it was loud.

Corey immediately appears back at the door. "What is your problem?"

I slam the door in his face. "None of your business!"

I stare at myself again. Yup, it's still there. Smack in the middle of my nose, a nasty red bump. Perfectly round, and totally nasty.

And not small.

I touch it. It hurts. I somehow resist the urge to claw at my face, because I remember hearing somewhere that if you do that, you could be scarred for life. Although a scar would be a lot better than this monstrosity plopped down in the middle of my nose.

I lean in closer. I can almost hear it laughing at me.

Hahahahahaha. Hey, Calista. Nice to meet you. It's me, Peter Pimple. Wanna be friends?

"NOOOOOO!" I run to my room, grab my phone, and fire off a group text to Ellie and Ella.

I FOUND A PIMPLE ON MY NOSE! WHAT DO I DO? HELP!!?!?

Five seconds later, I haven't heard back from either one of them, so I add: HELP!!!! I MEAN IT!!!!!

"Honey?" my mom calls from downstairs. "You coming down for breakfast?"

"I HAVE A PIMPLE ON MY NOSE!" I scream down to her. "A REAL ONE!"

"As opposed to a fake one?" she asks.

"I'M SERIOUS!"

I hear her sigh, then hear her footsteps on the stairs. She comes into the bathroom and grabs my head. "Let me see." She looks for two seconds, then says, "It's nothing. Don't touch it. It will be gone in a few days."

A few days?!??! I don't have a few days! I'm seeing Patrick Toole in forty-five minutes!

"I have to get ready for work, honey," says my mom,

and she goes back downstairs. So it's official: She doesn't love me.

My dad is no help either, of course, but luckily, my phone buzzes. It's Ella, texting back: OH NOOOOOO! HAVE YOU TRIED CONCEALER?

Hmmm. I don't use concealer. Probably because I've never had anything to conceal.

NO!!! I text back. I DON'T HAVE ANY!

Ella: YOUR MOM PROBABLY DOES

Me: GREAT IDEA!!!!

I run into my mom's bathroom and start searching for her concealer. When I find it, I dab some onto my nose. Then I dab some more. Eventually I dab a little too hard, and sure enough, the pimple pops.

YAY!

And also—NOOOOO!

Because a pool of blood starts to form where the pimple used to be.

EWWWWW!

I wipe my nose with a tissue for about two minutes, but it won't stop bleeding, so I find a bandage and put it over the cut. Then I go downstairs and try to act like nothing's wrong. But I start crying, which kills that idea.

My dad looks up from his phone. "Honey? What is it? Are you okay?"

Does it look like I'm okay?!?!?!

"I'm fine," I sniffle. "I just, uh . . . got a little cut on my nose."

"A what?" my dad asks, but before he can say any- thing else, my mom says, "Oh, she has a little pimple, but it's fine. You really don't need that bandage, you know. You're just going to draw more attention to it."

"I don't care," I mutter, leaving out the part about the concealer and the rubbing and the popping and the blood.

Corey giggles. "Little Miss Perfect has a pimple!"

"Knock it off!" I glare at him. "Just wait 'til you get pimples. You'll probably get a ton of them."

"Calista, that's enough," my mom barks.

"Fine!" I run upstairs, rub some more of my mom's concealer around my nose, then sprint out to the bus stop without saying goodbye to anyone.

LAURA

Everyone is always half-asleep for homeroom, which is why Ms. Harnick uses her outside voice. "Class!" she announces. "I need you to pay extra attention this morning. Class!" But she's not having much luck today, because people are focused on something else.

Extra, extra, read all about it! Calista Getz has a bandage on her nose!

And wait, there's more: She's also got a little blood that you can see peeking through the bandage, and some sort of weird brown powdery stuff on her cheeks that makes her look very strange. This is huge news, because her gorgeousness isn't usually marred by anything—even a bad hat.

When she first walked in, she stared straight ahead, with Ellie and Ella surrounding her, as if they were secret service agents and Calista was the president. People immediately noticed the bandage, of course, but no one said anything. No one dared.

Until just now, when Will Hanson whispers loud enough so that everyone can hear, "Cut yourself shaving?"

The class dissolves into giggles.

"Hush!" begs Ms. Harnick, but the damage is already done. The class is distracted. Game on.

"What did you say?" hisses Ellie to Will.

"Don't worry about it," Will says.

"Knock it off, Will," Patrick says, stepping in. Then he looks at Calista. "Hey, are you okay? What did happen, anyway?"

Everyone in the room turns to look at Calista, and once again we all see something we've never seen before.

She's blushing.

DAMIAN

This is pretty interesting.

Calista Getz is acting differently than she usually does.

Even our teacher, Ms. Harnick, seems just as fascinated as everyone else.

"No, I didn't cut myself shaving," Calista says, answering Will's stupid question. "But thank you for asking."

"Looks like you had a fight with a pimple and lost," says Simon Lippa, who is sitting right in front of Calista. It's surprising that Simon would have the nerve to speak to Calista, because he's pretty shy like me. Maybe it's because she has a bandage on her nose.

"You oughta know," Ellie says to Simon. "You look like you have plenty of experience with pimples."

Simon's face turns very red as he slouches down in his seat.

"So it's a pimple?" Will says. "Oh, cool! I wasn't sure Calista even knew what a pimple was!"

Now it's Calista's turn to blush again. "I know what a pimple is, now can we stop talking about it?"

"Hey, no biggie," Patrick said. "Everybody gets pimples, you know."

But that's the interesting part. Calista's not everybody. She's different from everybody. She's better.

Ms. Harnick claps her hands together. "Can we stop this conversation right now, please?"

"I just never saw you turn red before, is all," Patrick adds, which only makes Calista blush more.

I feel bad for her, which doesn't really make any sense.

I've had pimples before, and I'm pretty sure she's never felt bad for me.

CALISTA

Here is a math equation for you:

Sitting in class + A bandage on your nose = Forever.

Everyone gets pimples, Patrick had said.

I don't.

Homeroom feels like it's nine hours long. I'm not even sure what Ms. Harnick is talking about. My ears are burning, and I just want the class to end. But it won't end. Ever.

Until it finally does.

When the bell rings, I run down to the locker room to get ready for gym. Ellie and Ella are right behind me, yelling my name, but I pretend not to hear. I don't really want to talk to anyone right now. Especially those two. They are going to try and make me feel better, but they will end up making me feel worse. Friends are really good at that, for some reason.

"Callie, wait!"

That's a different voice.

I turn around, and Laura walks up to me. "Are you okay?"

"I'm fine, thanks."

"Will was just being dumb. And Patrick didn't mean to embarrass you—he was kind of flirting with you, that's all."

I smile. "Okay."

"I've had pimples before," Laura says. "They're annoying, but next time, don't pick it." She laughs. "Not that there will be a next time."

Ellie and Ella run up to us. I wish to myself that they would just go away.

"Calista!" Ellie says. "I hope you're telling Laura you're quitting soccer!"

Laura frowns. "What are you talking about?"

Ellie points at my face. "Your pimple! It's from sweat and dirt and all that gross stuff. Playing sports gives you pimples, everyone knows that."

"Look at all the other girls who play sports," echoes Ella. "Their faces, like, always break out."

That's the stupidest thing I've ever heard.

But for some reason, I look at Laura anyway.

LAURA

They all turn to me, and I touch my face.
I don't have any pimples, but I feel like I do.

CALISTA

"Laura doesn't have any pimples," I say. But just saying it makes me feel bad.

Laura's face gets red, and she walks away.

"Check again tomorrow," Ellie calls after her, and she and Ella laugh.

"Stop being such jerks," I say.

Ellie scowls. "What? That was funny."

"I'm going to go change," I say, "and I don't want to talk about this anymore. Or ever."

Which is true. I don't.

I just want to go to gym and run around.

Running around usually makes me feel better.

LAURA

We're doing basketball in gym. I love basketball—after soccer, it's my favorite sport.

The girls play on one half of the gym, the boys on the other.

We play a rotating tournament of three against three. On my team are this girl Jessica, who is really short and fast, and my friend Rachel from soccer, who is great at blocking shots. I'm a good shooter. (Again with the bragging! I'm sorry!) Together, we're a pretty solid team. We make it to the finals of the tournament, where we end up playing against Calista, Ellie, and Ella. Ellie and Ella are terrible athletes and seem to enjoy being terrible, but Calista is one of the best basketball players I've ever seen. She doesn't miss. And she doesn't even like basketball that much, according to her.

My team shakes hands with Calista's team before the game. When I shake with Calista, I notice that her face and neck are really red. But she's been sweating a lot, so maybe it's just that.

"Let's do this," she says.

I nod. "Let's."

"Just don't hurt me, deal?" she adds. She's referring back to soccer practice last night, but she's smiling when she says it.

"Depends on the score," I answer, and we both laugh. It's strange to laugh with her. It feels like a memory.

The game starts, and right away I notice that Calista is wiping her face a lot. Then she starts scratching it. At first I think it's just sweat that's annoying her.

"Callie, are you okay?" I ask her.

"I'm fine," she says, blowing past me for a lay-up.

But she keeps wiping her face, and as the game goes on, her face starts changing colors. It goes from tan, to red, to deep red.

And then I remember what Ellie said: *Playing sports gives you pimples.*

Jeez, turns out she was right.

CALISTA

At first, it feels like I have a mosquito bite, then like I have ten mosquito bites, then like nothing I've ever felt before. I get a hot, tingling sensation. And every time I try to scratch the itch, it gets worse.

Finally, I stop running. I hunch over to catch my breath and feel Mr. Decker, the gym teacher, staring down at me.

"Everything all right?"

I look up at him and immediately his face changes.

"Oh," he says. But not the good kind of "oh." The bad kind of "oh."

"You should probably . . . uh . . . go get that looked at, Calista."

By now, all the other girls are looking at me, and it feels like Ms. Harnick's class all over again, only more embarrassing, because I know my face looks worse. I can't see it, but I feel it.

I run straight to the nurse's office.

Gym is my least favorite class.

I'm actually pretty coordinated. I used to be a good hitter in little league, and because I'm tall, I'm definitely one of the better basketball players.

But I stopped playing organized sports a while ago. It was just easier that way.

I have to go to gym, though. I can't get out of it. I tried. My parents talked to the school and everything. My doctor even wrote a note. Eventually we came to a compromise and the school said I had to go for half of gym class and then when it got too uncomfortable I could go to the nurse's office and get changed. So after scoring twelve points in fifteen minutes (like I said, I'm tall), that's exactly what I do.

After changing into a new shirt, I sit down on one of the beds and start doing my homework. Nurse Kline leaves me alone, and it's quiet, as usual. In all the time

I've been coming to the nurse's office, I've barely ever seen another person, unless you count Dave Eckert, who gets the flu practically every other week.

Today, though, is different.

I'm working on vocabulary—trying to memorize the definition of the word "enigma"—when the door opens and Calista Getz walks in.

It takes me exactly two seconds to realize she's crying.

Nurse Kline, who is reading something on her computer, jerks her head up like she just heard a bomb go off.

"Calista!" At first, I'm surprised she knows Calista's name. But then I remember everyone knows Calista's name.

Calista doesn't answer. Instead, she hops up on the other bed. She has a gym towel wrapped around her head.

"What's wrong?" asks Nurse Kline. She gently tries to remove the towel, and after a few seconds Calista lets her take it.

She has a bad rash covering half her face.

It's red, and splotchy, and it's the absolute last thing you would ever expect to see on a face as perfect as Calista Getz's.

"Oh, my," says the nurse. "Looks like a nasty case of hives, or some sort of allergic reaction."

"I know!" Calista moans. "Can you do something? Can you help me?"

"We can take care of that, don't you worry. It will be

gone in a day or two, at the most." Nurse Kline goes off to look for what she needs. Calista sighs and sniffles, then looks over and notices me for the first time. She doesn't look happy to see me. She probably wants to be alone. I wouldn't blame her.

But she smiles.

"Hey," she says. "Damian, right?"

I almost fall off the bed.

"Um, yes."

"Hi. Did you have a good summer? I saw you yesterday in the cafeteria."

Speaking is difficult, but I manage to say four words. "I saw you, too."

Nurse Kline returns with some cream that she starts spreading on Calista's face. "Any idea how this might have happened?" she asks.

Calista glances at me, then takes a deep breath. "I . . . um . . . I found a pimple on my nose this morning. And, and I didn't know what to do. One of my friends told me to use some of my mom's concealer to cover it up. And, um, maybe when I sweated in gym, it combined with that."

The nurse keeps wiping. "Lots of things can cause allergic reactions. In any case, the best advice for pimples is to leave them alone."

"Everyone keeps telling me that," Calista whimpers.

"That's because it's good advice." Nurse Kline checks her watch. "We need to give the cream a little time to work. I have to run down to the principal's office to pick up some paperwork. I'll be back in two minutes."

Then she goes out.

Which leaves just the two of us.

Me and Calista.

CALISTA

After thirty or forty uncomfortable seconds, I decide to break the silence. If I wait for Damian, the silence will never break.

"Are you still drawing a lot?"

Damian looks like he's seen a ghost. "Huh?"

"I remember when we first met," I tell him. "You had like, a big drawing pad in your hands."

He blinks five times in two seconds. "I did?"

"Yup. Last year, when you just moved here, Dr. Michener asked me to show you around. Do you remember?"

Damian looks at me as if I've just asked the stupidest question in the world, which I suppose I have.

"Yes. I remember. And, uh, yes, I still like to draw."

"Great. Well, it's nice to see you again."

"What do you mean?" Damian asks. "You saw me at lunch yesterday."

"Right," I say. "I just meant, it's nice to talk to you again."

"Oh," Damian says. "It's nice to talk to you again, too."

Nurse Kline comes back. "Let's take a look," she says. I move my hand away from my face. "Ah. Much better." She pats me encouragingly on the knee. "Go take a look!"

I glance over at Damian, who smiles. I walk over to the mirror and make myself look. The hives aren't much better, if you ask me. I still look like an iguana.

I look back at the nurse. "Now what?"

"Now you go back to class," she says gently. "I believe your grade is at lunch?"

I hesitate.

"You don't look that bad," Damian says. "I've seen worse rashes on other people."

"Not helpful!" I say, but Damian's sweet honesty makes me feel a tiny bit better. I grab my backpack and head toward the door, but stop to ask Damian one last question. "I meant to ask you—why are you in the nurse's office?"

He shrugs. "Oh, you know—the usual."

I don't know what that means, but before I can ask, he lies back down on the bed, and it's clear he doesn't want to talk about it.

"Thank you, Nurse Kline," I say, and head out the door.

The lunch room is fifty feet away.

I wish it were a thousand.

LAURA

The first thing I notice at lunch is that Patrick is talking to Ellie, which isn't too surprising. But the second thing I notice is that Ellie is sitting in Calista's usual seat, and that's shocking. Even though Calista isn't there, this is a big deal, because that's like sitting on the queen's throne. Calista decided she liked that seat last year, and that was that. No one ever questioned it, and no one else ever sat in it, until today.

I guess Ellie thought Calista was spending the whole lunch period in the nurse's office.

Uh, she was wrong.

Calista walks in, and all her friends look up, shocked. Patrick quickly hustles back to his table. When Calista notices Ellie in her seat, she stops in her tracks. After a few seconds, Ellie decides to get up. They all take their usual seats, including Calista.

Everything seems back to normal, but it's not.

Something's changed. I can tell.

DAMIAN

A few minutes after Calista leaves the nurse's office, I put my jacket on and head down to the cafeteria, too. I notice Calista and almost say hi to her but don't, because we're not in the nurse's office anymore. I can talk to her in the nurse's office, but not anywhere else, really.

I head to my table in the back, where Jeffrey is sitting alone.

"Hey, Jeffrey."

"Hey, Damian."

I take out my lunch bag and my drawing pad. I tell myself not to look up at all during lunch. Especially not in Calista's direction.

Two minutes later, I look up.

LAURA

I'm still watching Calista and her friends when Rachel elbows me in the shoulder.

"Why do you waste your time worrying about them?" she says. "It's so not worth it."

I look at Rachel, wondering what to say. Rachel became my new best friend when Calista and I kind of went our separate ways, and I think she always worries a little bit that I would run back to Calista if I could. But otherwise, Rachel is the most cheerful person I know. She's loud and big and doesn't seem to care at all about who's cool and who's hot and who's popular and stuff like that.

I totally wish I were more like her.

"Calista's my friend," I say.

"Whatever you say, dear," says Rachel. "Oh, and P.S., you're staring."

This time I don't answer. I know she's right. But it doesn't matter.

I can still remember the minute my relationship with Calista changed. We were in fifth grade. Calista was over at my house after school one day, and we were having cereal in the kitchen when my brother Eddie came in. He was two years older than me and thought all my friends were losers. He thought Calista was a loser too, until that day.

Eddie looked at Calista. "Hey, Callie. What are you guys up to?"

I dropped my spoon in my bowl.

Calista glanced at me before answering. "Uh, not much. We were going to maybe shoot baskets or something. Right, Laurasaurus?"

"Right," I said.

"Sounds fun," Eddie said. "Maybe I'll shoot some baskets with you."

That was when I knew.

CALISTA

I don't say anything to Patrick as he walks by. I guess I'm still getting over the shock of Ellie sitting in my seat. And also, I have a face full of hives, so there's that. Once I sit down, though, the curiosity gets the better of me.

"What were you guys talking about with Patrick?" I ask.

Ellie and Ella look at each other.

"Nothing," says Ellie.

"Seriously, nothing," adds Ella.

"Wow, Calista, you look so much better," Camille says. "I can only see the rash, like, on half your face. In gym, it was covering the whole thing."

Did I say earlier that I appreciated Camille's honesty? I take it back.

"Gee, thanks." Everything is fine, I think, trying to convince myself.

I take a bite of my salad, as Ellie says something to

Ella that I can't hear. "No seriously, what were you guys talking about?" I ask again. They glance up at me.

"Oh, hahaha, just stupid stuff," Ellie says.

"Totally dumb," Ella says.

I feel my rash start to tingle. "What stupid stuff?"

Ellie turns her eyes in my direction and for the first time ever she looks irritated with me. "Just stupid dance stuff, that's all."

"What about the dance?" I say, unable to stop myself.

Everyone at the table stops talking, and it feels like the whole cafeteria is looking at me, even though I know they're not.

"Is Patrick still going to ask me?" I'm thinking it, so I may as well say it out loud and get it over with.

Ellie tries to look shocked. "Why wouldn't he?"

"Uh, have you looked at me lately? I have a pimple on my nose and lizard skin all over my face."

"Jeez, Calista," says Ella. "Do you really think Patrick is, like, that shallow?"

"I don't know," I say. "That's why I'm asking you."

"Why would you want to go with someone who might change their mind about you, just because of how you look?" asks Camille, from the other end of the table.

Heads swivel in her direction.

"Who asked you?" I say to Camille. It comes out mean, I know, but I can't help it.

"Patrick totally likes you for you," Ellie reassures me.

"Ha," I say.

"If you don't think so, why don't you go ask him?" Ella says.

"Maybe I will." I can barely stand listening to myself. Are we really talking about this?

I stand up and walk over to Patrick's table. He's in the middle of looking at some dumb video on his phone with Will and Jason, another one of his friends. They see me coming before he does. They elbow him, and he looks up at me.

"Oh, hey," he says. "Uh, how's your face?" I notice his eyes are looking past me, at someone else. He seems uncomfortable, and I think I know why.

"It's just fantastic," I say. "Can't you tell?"

He laughs awkwardly.

I can feel my heart pounding. "So, uh, did you have something you wanted to ask me?"

I wait for what seems like three hours.

"Calista, about the dance, I—" he finally says, but that's as far as he gets before I cut him off.

"No, I get it. You don't have to explain."

But he explains anyway. "I'm just confused, I guess. I heard you weren't going to the dance anyway—you know, with your rash and everything—"

"Gee, I wonder where you heard that." I glare back at Ellie and Ella, then turn back to Patrick. "Did you ask someone else?" I hate myself for sounding so pathetic.

"No, of course not!" His eyes dart all over the place, anywhere but in my direction. "Uh, if you still want to go, I guess we could still go, you know, if you really want to."

"Don't worry about it. Seriously, Patrick, it's fine." I look around, trying to find someone to talk to, somewhere to go that's not back at my table. I spot Damian at the far end of the cafeteria, staring at me. When I look at him, he looks away, of course.

"I, uh, need to go talk to my friend," I say, and I find myself turning in Damian's direction.

Will Hanson grabs my arm. "Calista, hold up. I hope you're not still mad at that dumb shaving joke."

"Actually," I say, "I thought it was pretty funny."

I walk away and don't look back.

DAMIAN

"Oh, man," Jeffrey says.

I try not to look up from my drawing. "What?"

"Calista is looking at you, and she's coming this way."

"Ha-ha."

"No seriously, she is."

I drop my pencil and lift my head up. Jeffrey's right. Calista is walking straight toward us.

"Oh, man," Jeffrey repeats. "Oh man oh man oh man oh man."

"Stop saying that," I tell him. I feel my shirt start to dampen.

"Oh, man," he says again, anyway. "What is she doing? Maybe she likes you. Maybe she wants to talk to you some more. Maybe she wants to go to the dance with you. You should ask her."

"Please stop talking now, Jeffrey."

"Okay."

I think about Jeffrey's annoying words. She was

really friendly in the nurse's office—she smiled at me even though she had a rash on her face. She remembered me.

And she's coming my way.

I could never ask her to the dance. But I could talk to her, and that would be nice, and maybe we could be friends—

Calista is almost at our table.

I suddenly stand up. "Okay. I will talk to her."

"Hey!" Jeffrey says, pointing at my shirt. I look down—it's drenched. It's covered in sweat stains. Especially under the arms. "Put your jacket back on," he suggests.

"Good idea."

I lean down over my chair and try to pull my jacket on, but one of the sleeves is inside out. I try to fix it, but I'm in a rush and make it worse. Suddenly both arms are inside out and I'm trying to pull the jacket on over my head. My arms are flailing around and my head is stuck inside the jacket and I can't see anything and I start to panic and I get one arm in and I'm still struggling with the other arm and I finally get it through and—

SMACK!!!

I feel my elbow hit something soft. It feels like a person. The sound isn't loud, but it's powerful. Like a combination of a crack and a smush. I hear a startled cry and then a moan. I finish pulling on my jacket.

The first thing I see is Calista Getz, with blood pouring out of her nose.

CALISTA

I stand there in shock, like I know what just happened but refuse to believe it. I put my hand up to my face and feel the blood.

Tears spring to my eyes but for some reason they don't come out. I think they're tears of pain, because all of a sudden, it really, really hurts.

Damian is also standing there in shock, unable to move, but the other boy at the table jumps up. "Oh, my gosh! Are you okay?"

My hands are still covering my face. "Could you maybe hand me those napkins?"

"Of course!"

Everyone in the cafeteria has stopped talking. I can hear the silence, and the humming of the soda machine. The pain starts spreading through my face, and I lash out at Damian. "What is wrong with you? You just smacked me in the face! Are you crazy?"

He slowly sinks down into his chair. "Oh, boy," he says. "Oh, boy."

I hear footsteps and look up to see Laura running up to the table.

"Mr. Decker is getting ice," she tells me. She looks at my face. "Does it hurt? It doesn't look that bad, I swear."

I don't say anything, so Laura adds, "I'm serious, it's doesn't look bad. Want me to take you to the bathroom so you can see for yourself?"

"No!" I say immediately. "I'm scared to look in a mirror. It might shatter into a million pieces." I glance at Damian, who looks slightly relieved that I'm able to make a little joke.

"Ha!" Laura says, sitting down next to me. "You never have to be scared to look in a mirror."

I'm starting to calm down. "Even with a pimple, a rash, and a bloody nose?"

She nods. "Yup. Even with all that."

It's amazing how one friendly person can make you feel better.

"That's a nice thing to say," I tell her, but she's not looking at me anymore.

"Oh, great," she says, "here comes the Goon Squad."

I have no idea what that means, until I see Ellie and Ella come running up.

"Are you okay?" Ellie says. "What was that about?"

Laura rolls her eyes. "Seriously? Her nose just got smashed and is bleeding, is what that was about."

"I wasn't talking to you." Ellie sneers while Ella shoots daggers at Laura with her eyes.

"I need a favor," I say. "Can one of you guys grab my backpack and bring it to the nurse's office?"

"Sure, yeah," Ellie says. She looks at Ella. "Actually, can you? I told Melanie I would walk down to the computer lab with her."

Ella fidgets on her feet. "Yup! I just have to go over the cheers with Becky, but I'll be down after—"

"Don't worry, I got it," Laura interrupts.

Ella glares at Laura again. "I'd said I'd do it!" She turns back to me. "Just give me a minute."

"This isn't about you," Laura says to Ella. "You didn't just have someone break your nose."

"Is it broken?" Damian asks with a panicky voice. "Oh, no! Did I break it?"

"It's okay!" I snap at him. "How many times do I have to tell you!"

He shrinks back in his chair, and immediately I feel terrible. I hate the way Ellie and Ella can rile me up. "You two just need to leave me alone for a while," I tell them.

"Who needs ice?" Mr. Decker asks, as he walks up with an ice pack and an overly-chipper smile. "Youch, you've got a bit of a doozy there," he says, placing the ice on my nose. "But you'll be good as new in no time!" He looks around. "Who can walk her down to the nurse?"

Before anyone else can answer, Damian stands up.

"I will. It's the least I can do."

"Great," says Mr. Decker. He hands me the ice pack. "Keep it on, light pressure, until you get down there."

"Okay, Mr. Decker, thanks." My voice sounds nasally and hoarse—as bad as my face probably looks.

I slowly get up. "Thanks for offering," I tell Laura, "but Damian can grab my backpack." Then to Ellie and Ella, I add, "Thanks for nothing."

As I walk past them, Ellie mumbles to Ella, "No wonder Patrick didn't ask her to the dance. One little boo-boo and she starts acting like a witch."

I pretend not to hear.

My heartbeat is still racing as Calista and I walk toward the nurse's office.

"I'm such an idiot," I mumble. "I'm really sorry."

"You're not an idiot," Calista says. "I don't get what you were doing with that stupid jacket, though. Why were you in such a rush to put it on?"

"I like having it on," I tell her.

"Why? Are you, like, always cold or something?"

"I didn't want you to see me without it." I take a deep breath and realize it's now or never. "I have something called hyperhidrosis. It means you sweat way more than the average person. You basically never stop sweating. Most people just think I sweat a lot because I'm nervous. I can control it with medicine sometimes but when I'm really stressed out it gets bad, and I totally sweat through my shirts. Like now."

She looks over at me, but I can't really see her face

because of the ice. "So that's why you always wear the jacket?"

I nod.

"Oh."

Nurse Kline is waiting at the door. "Back so soon, Calista? Gee, you must have really missed me." She guides Calista to a chair. "I heard about what happened. Let me take a quick look." She feels around Calista's face, but Calista doesn't make a sound. I'm impressed with how brave she's being.

The nurse gets a new ice pack. "Well as far as I can tell, sweetheart, it's not broken."

"Yay," Calista says, weakly. "That's good, right?"

"Better than a stick in the eye. And bad things happen in threes, so this should be it for a while." Nurse Kline turns to me, as if just noticing I was there. "Is this all your fault?"

"It was an accident," Calista says, quickly.

Nurse Kline laughs. "Oh, Damian knows I'm just messing with him. We're old friends."

I nod. "I come in here when I need to change shirts," I tell Calista. "One or two times a day. I can only make it through half of gym class before I have to change. Nurse Kline lets me hang out here."

"Not for long," says the nurse. "The hyperhidrosis medicine is really starting to do its job. Soon enough you'll be able to join the basketball team if you want."

"Okay." I sit in a chair next to the scale, suddenly feeling really tired. "You're a really good athlete, Calista," I say. "I've seen you play soccer and basketball. You're as good as the boys."

Calista tries to smile. "Thanks, I guess."

"What do you mean, you guess?"

"I don't know."

"Don't you love sports?"

"I don't know."

She walks over to the mirror and stares at herself.

"I don't know anything anymore," she says.

CALISTA

There it all is, staring me in the face.

An ugly gash from where I popped the pimple. A rash that runs from my cheeks to my chin. A swollen nose. Two dark circles under my eyes.

"Wow, I look fantastic," I say, staring in the mirror. Then I turn back to Nurse Kline. "I need to go home. Like, now."

The nurse nods. "I've already talked to your mom," she says. "She's on her way. You can text her if you want, I won't tell." Normally there's no texting during school, but there was nothing normal about what was happening to me.

I take out my phone. MOM! HOW SOON WILL YOU BE HERE. HURRY PLEEEEEEZ THIS HAS BEEN THE WORST DAY EVER

Ten seconds later she texts back: HI HONEY, I'M SO SORRY!! THE NURSE CALLED A FEW MIN AGO. I'M

LEAVING WORK ASAP AND CAN BE THERE BY 1. BTW WE CAN STILL GO TO THE MALL IF YOU WANT

I immediately text back: HAHAHAHAHAHAHA NO WAY ☺

OK, texts my mom. UP TO YOU. MIGHT BE FUN DISTRACTION THO? ☺

I'm not really in the mood for happy faces. I CAN'T EVEN THINK ABOUT THAT RIGHT NOW, I text. WE'LL TALK ABOUT IT WHEN U GET HERE.

I put my phone away and lie back on the bed. "I'm supposed to get a dress today, for the dance," I tell the ceiling.

"Oh," Damian answers. A few seconds later, he adds, "Who are you going with?"

"Can't decide," I say. "I'm fighting them off with a stick."

"That's great," Damian says.

"I was kidding."

"Oh."

I look over at him. He's got a new shirt on, light yellow, with that red jacket over it.

"If you want to be friends with me, you don't have to punch me in the nose, you know. You can just ask me like a normal person. And you need to get rid of that silly jacket."

"I like this jacket," Damian says. "It's my favorite jacket."

I shake my head and close my eyes. The next thing I know, there's a tap on my shoulder. Nurse Kline is looking down at me. I glance over at the other table, but Damian is gone.

"How long have I been asleep?"

"A half hour," the nurse says. "The swelling's gone down, and your hives are looking a bit better, too. So, as much as I'd like to let you sleep the day away, I think you can go back to class until your mom gets here."

"What?" I immediately protest. "Why?"

"Because last I checked," she says, "this was still a school, and you're still a student."

I love books. (Dweeb alert.)

I love losing myself in stories and escaping to different places. Sometimes you just need to get away from real life for a little while, you know?

When I was younger, my mom used to love that I loved reading. "My little genius," she'd say. But then something changed as I got older. I would be in my room with a book and she'd come in and say something like, "Isn't your brain tired?" Sometimes she would pretend to give me a compliment or try to say something nice, like "I bet you're the only girl in the whole school who's spending a Saturday night working like a busy beaver! You're amazing!" I don't think she knew that what she really meant was, "Why aren't you having a slumber party with friends?"

When I met Calista, we realized we had two things in common: soccer and reading. At first, we loved doing both together. But then, slowly, Calista lost interest in the reading part. She decided it was boring and wanted to do other stuff with her new friends. Then she started asking if she could copy my homework, and I said yes. Last year we were in different English classes, so she stopped asking.

But this year, we wound up in the same class, with a teacher named Mr. Cody. Everyone says he's nice but tough. And so far it seems like everyone's right, since yesterday he told us that there are going to be three quizzes and two tests this quarter, plus homework three nights a week.

We're in the middle of discussing the summer reading assignment when the door to the classroom opens. Everyone turns to look as Calista walks in, with her head down. Her face is pretty much a total mess. A couple of kids giggle, which is gross.

"Hello!" calls out Mr. Cody. He looks down at his attendance sheet. "Welcome, Ms. Getz."

"I'm sorry I'm late," Calista says, quietly.

"Quite all right," says Mr. Cody. "I've gotten the full report. You're feeling okay?"

"My mom is picking me up in a half hour," Calista answers, which isn't exactly an answer. "I just want to go home."

"I understand completely." Mr. Cody sits on the edge of his desk. "We've been discussing the summer reading assignment this morning, and I'm hoping you might want to join the conversation. Do you have any thoughts on *The Curious Incident of the Dog in the Night-time*?"

The class waits while Calista fumbles with her backpack.

"Uh . . ."

Mr. Cody smiles. "'Uh' is a promising beginning," he says, and the class laughs. "What else ya got?"

Calista tries to muster up her most adorable smile— the one that has charmed teachers for the last five years.

"I—I thought it was really good." Her eyes suddenly find me. "Laura and I read it together, on her screen porch," she says. "We loved it, didn't we?"

All eyes suddenly turn to me. For a second I feel torn between defending my friend and lying. Guess which won. "Uh . . . yeah, we totally did love it," I say.

"Right!" Calista says. "It was so awesome!"

The only problem is, Mr. Cody is no dummy.

"I'm so glad you liked it," he says to Calista. "That's great. What did you think of the present Christopher's father gives him at the end of the book?"

Calista's rash seems to take a sudden turn for the worse. She starts twirling the hair behind her left ear, which is a nervous habit she's had ever since she was a little girl.

"Uh . . . I didn't quite get to that part." She sinks back in her chair.

"Did you get to any part of the book?"

"I guess not."

"Ah, I see," says Mr. Cody. "Well, because of your trying day, we'll give you a pass on your little fib." He turns his eyes to me. "Can you please tell us what the present was?"

"A puppy," I say, in not much more than a whisper.

Mr. Cody nods. "I don't tolerate lying in my classroom. I know you're just trying to protect your friend, but sometimes loyalty becomes stupidity. Don't let it happen again."

"I'm very sorry," I mumble.

"Okay then." Mr. Cody moves his eyes around the class. "Is there anyone else who 'didn't quite get to it,' to coin a phrase?"

Five or six hands reluctantly inch up—including Will Hanson's, of course.

"Well, excellent," Mr. Cody says. "Because I love company, and tomorrow you'll all be keeping me company in our exciting after-school study hall. And you'll keep on keeping me company until you finish the book." He grins. "Doesn't that sound like fun?"

The various moans and groans heard around the classroom give him the only answer he needs.

"Great!" he chirps. "Now, where were we?"

CALISTA

My ears are making the same buzzing sound they made when I first walked into the classroom and everyone stared at me. I'm used to people looking at me, of course. But this isn't that. This is something completely different. This is people pretending not to look at me, or trying not to look at me, but looking at me anyway.

My heart is pounding, and my blood is racing, which makes the swelling in my face throb. I can feel the rash pricking my skin. I bury my head in my notebook and start writing my name a thousand different ways. Calista GETZ. CALISTA Getz! Calitsa R. Getz. Ms. Calista Getz.

I meant to read the book, I really did. I always mean to. I like to read! I used to read a lot. I don't know what happened, I guess I just got really busy with other stuff. I'm usually able to catch up later. Teachers don't usually care that much, as long as you get the work done, but Mr. Cody is obviously different.

I'm different, too—as of this morning.

I raise my hand, and Mr. Cody stops talking.

"Yes, Calista?"

"May I go wait in the office for my mother to pick me up? I'm really not feeling well."

He nods. "Sure, you can get a head start on the reading. I'll see you tomorrow." He throws me a copy of the book, and I catch it. "We'll have lots of quality time together," he adds.

The class laughs, which makes me mad for a second, but then I realize what he said was actually funny.

"I can't wait," I say, and the class laughs again, at my joke.

As I walk out, I realize that the laughter makes me feel something I haven't felt all day.

Better.

DAMIAN

Calista leaves the class with a slight smile on her face.

"Who else actually *did* read the book?" Mr. Cody asks.

I raise my hand, which is something that doesn't usually happen.

"Yes, uh . . ." He looks at his sheet for my name. ". . . Damian?"

"I read it," I say.

"And?"

"I really liked it." I pause, before deciding to add more. "I really liked the kid, Christopher. He was different but it didn't bother him."

Mr. Cody paces the aisles of the classroom, tapping his pen on his chin. "What do you mean, exactly?"

"I mean, he had a job to do and he did it. He didn't care if other people thought it was strange. He believed in himself and what he was doing and that was all that mattered."

"You see?" Mr. Cody says loudly. "THIS is what can happen when you do the assigned reading. Coherent thoughts can form in your head, and you can actually speak in complete sentences that are interesting and perceptive. Can you imagine?"

The class laughs. This guy Mr. Cody is pretty funny. I see Calista's friend Laura looking at me. I turn away but quickly turn back, and she's still looking. Then she raises her hand.

"Yes, uh . . . Laura, the friend protector?"

She blushes as the class laughs again. "I agree with Damian. And also, Christopher had a real sense of right and wrong. He saw a crime and he wasn't sure anyone else was going to do anything about it, and he decided that wasn't right, so he decided to solve it. His strength and determination were kind of noble in a way, I guess. I thought that was pretty cool."

"I agree," says Mr. Cody. "I also thought that was pretty cool."

Laura smiles at me. I smile back.

I can't remember a girl ever smiling like that at me before.

I also can't remember anything else that happens in the rest of the class.

LAURA

After class, I wait in the hallway for Damian to come out. I see his red jacket before I see him, and before I know it he's past me. I hurry to catch up.

"Hey," I say.

He barely glances over at me, and I can feel his nervousness. Boys don't usually get nervous around me. It feels nice.

"Hey," he says. "That was nice, what you did for Calista."

"I almost got in trouble for it."

"I know."

"I'm Laura."

"I know."

I pause for a second, then say, "I hope you're not blaming yourself for what happened to Calista's face. It wasn't your fault."

"I bashed her nose with my elbow," Damian says, more to the floor than to me.

"Yeah, but it was a total accident."

"Her other friends didn't seem to want to help her very much."

"Well, they're jerks," I say, before I can stop myself.

Damian stops walking and really looks at me for the first time. "Why are her friends jerks?"

"I shouldn't have said that," I say. Then I let out a small laugh. "I don't know. They just are. They specialize in jerkiness."

We start walking again. "They're in all the honors jerkiness classes," Damian says. "And they're great students!" He laughs loudly at his own joke, which is fine by me.

"Will Hanson is in that class, too," I add, which makes Damian tense up. I sense I've crossed a line.

"Will isn't a jerk, he's just mean," he says.

"I'm sorry," I say quickly. "I shouldn't have said that. I've seen how Will talks to you. He really, truly is the worst."

"Yeah he is."

Damian and I walk for another minute or two, not saying anything.

"I have to go," Damian says, stopping in front of the nurse's office. "I'm a little sick."

"Okay," I say, offering him a quick smile. "See you later. It was really nice meeting you."

"It was really nice meeting you, too."

As he opens the door and goes in, I read the back of his jacket: RENEGADES. Funny, I've seen that red jacket ever since Damian moved here, but I never noticed that before. For a second I wonder who the Renegades are, then I forget about it and go to my next class.

CALISTA

"Calista, your mom's here."

I'm reading *The Curious Incident* in the main office when I look up to see Dr. Michener, the principal, standing over me. She bends down. "Want some help?"

"I'm okay, thanks."

When I get up I feel the blood rush to my face, making my whole head throb. My mom gets buzzed in through the front door, then breaks into a run when she sees me. I can tell by her eyes that she's a little shocked.

"Honey," she says. "Calista. Come here."

She holds her arms out and I fall into them and my body sags against hers and I feel incredibly tired.

My mom gently pushes me back and stands me up. "Let me look at you." I see her eyes scanning my face, searching for every mark and imperfection. "Oh, it's not so bad!" she says, lying through her teeth. "Is it true, you tried my concealer? To hide that pimple?"

I glance at Nurse Kline, who is also standing there. I'm mad that she told my mom, but I don't blame her. That's her job.

"I—I wasn't sure what else to do."

"That's crazy." She takes my face in her hands. "You're a beautiful girl. A beautiful girl. One little blemish is never going to change that." She turns my head a little bit to the side. "Your nose got a nice whack. Holy smokes."

"The boy who did it feels horrible," I tell my mom.

"He oughta," she says.

Dr. Michener steps forward. "We'll see you tomorrow, Calista?"

"I guess so," I say. "If I feel better."

"She'll be fine," my mom says. "It's nothing that a little nap can't cure." Then she looks at me and whispers, "And then a quick trip to the mall."

I stare at her. "The mall? You were serious?"

"Yup. We'll get some of those cinnamon buns you love; it'll be just what the doctor ordered." She grabs my hand, and we start walking to the car. "Plus, we've got a dress to buy."

CALISTA

My mom takes me home, where I immediately fall asleep for an hour and a half. As soon as I wake up, I remember everything that happened during the day, and I pull the blanket up over my head. But my mom hears me and is in my room in five seconds.

"Ready?"

"No."

"Good. We're leaving in ten minutes."

Ugh.

I argue with my mom for the next nine minutes, but there's no point. We're going to the mall, and that's that. I think it's because she wants to keep me distracted, and to get me out of the bathroom, where I'd just stare in the mirror at my broken face all day.

On the way there, my mom keeps asking me questions—"So tell me about the kid who elbowed you?" "What time did you get the rash?" "Which friend told you to use the concealer?"—but I don't want to talk about it. I mumble one-word answers. Finally, she changes the subject.

"What kind of dress do you want? Is this a formal dance?"

"Uh . . ." I say, which is not the answer she's looking for.

"What, honey?"

"Um, actually, I'm not sure I'm going to the dance?" I say it as a question, probably because I know my mom will have an answer.

"Of course you're going," she says in that tone of voice that means this is not up for discussion. Then, just to eliminate any possible confusion, she adds, "This is not up for discussion."

The mall isn't very crowded, so we get a parking space near the door. It's starting to rain, and I get paranoid that the wetness will make my hives flare up again, so I run inside and head straight to the little store that sells my favorite cinnamon buns. Every time I go to the mall I get one. It's like a reflex. My mom comes in a minute later, and we sit across from each other, eating in silence. It's nice. I feel my body start to relax, just a little bit.

Then I hear a voice I recognize. "Callie?"

I turn around and try to smile.

"Hey, Laura. What are you doing here?"

She looks self-conscious, like she's searching for a lie,

but she decides to go for the truth. "Getting a dress for the dance."

"It's so good to see you, Laura!" blurts out my mom. "We're getting a dress, too. Do you want to shop with us?"

"Sure," Laura says. "Sounds great."

I shoot my mom a look.

Sometimes parents just don't get it.

LAURA

"I'm going to get a coffee," Calista's mom tells us. "You girls get started without me. I'll be there in a few."

We head into the store.

"I really appreciate you having my back with Mr. Cody today," Calista tells me. "I'm sorry I put you on the spot like that."

"No worries," I say. Then I add, "That's what friends are for," slipping in a little dig at Ellie and Ella.

"For sure," Calista says. I can't tell if she gets my extra meaning. "Thanks again."

"I'm meeting Rachel here," I tell her. Calista nods without saying anything. I'm pretty sure she's not in the mood for a social gathering. "We don't have to hang out, if you don't want," I add.

"No, it'll be fun," she says, trying to be a good sport.

Two saleswomen come up to us. "Can we help you ladies?" they say, even though neither one of them looks at me. They're both totally focusing on Calista. Her face might be a little bit of a mess, but she's still the main attraction.

"I'm looking for a dress," I say, but I can't seem to get their attention. *Hello, I'm over here!* "We have a dance this weekend, and I would prefer not to embarrass myself and others."

Finally the saleswomen notice me. "Excuse me?" says one of the women, as if I'm speaking French.

"Let's do this!" I say. "Make me gorgeous! Find me something hot!" The snobby saleswomen laugh, and we all relax.

Hey, if you can't get them with beauty, get them with comedy, am I right?

CALISTA

Laura tries on five dresses before I even try on one. She's having a blast, twirling around in front of the mirror, acting silly. When Rachel gets here, they hold pretend microphones, singing made-up songs at the top of their lungs. They seem so happy.

"How about you?" The two salespeople stand in front of me, each with two dresses in their hands. "Ready to try these on?"

"Don't you want to finish up with them first?" I say, pointing at Laura and Rachel.

One of the women shakes her head. "Oh, they're fine," she says. "We'll check back with them in a few minutes." To be honest, I'm used to the sales staff at clothing stores fawning over me. Usually I don't really even notice it, but today I do.

I'm trying on the third dress when my mom comes back. "I love it!" she says. "It fits your body perfectly."

"Great," I say. "I'll take it." I hurry back into the dressing room and take it off. Through the curtain I can hear Laura and Rachel cracking up about something. I walk into their dressing room and they're standing there in their underwear, each holding a dress in front of them, making faces in the mirror. It occurs to me that if I had the same body type that they do, I might be a little self-conscious about anybody else seeing it. But there they are, having the time of their lives. Amazing.

They look up and notice me.

"Calista!" Laura exclaims. "Check out our dresses! Did you find something?"

"Yeah, I guess."

Rachel starts putting her clothes on. "Did you look stunning?" she says. "As stunning as us?"

"Ha!" Laura howls.

Rachel smacks her on the butt. "What? We're totally gorgeous, and don't you forget it!"

Laura also starts dressing. "So, see you at soccer later?" she asks me.

"I don't know," I say, before realizing I'm saying it. "I don't think so."

They both stare at me.

"Huh?" says Laura.

"I don't think I'm coming," I say.

"What do you mean?" Laura asks. "Even if you can't practice today, you're still supposed to come and be with the team."

"It's not that," I say. "I actually don't think I'm going to play this year."

The air in the room changes as their moods darken.

"Are you kidding?" Laura asks. "Of course you're playing. You're like, one of the best players. You played amazing in practice yesterday. We need you."

Rachel rolls her eyes. "This happens all the time with pretty girls," she says. "Did someone tell you that sports aren't ladylike? Is that it?"

"Not at all," I say.

"Actually, someone did," Laura says. "I was there."

Rachel puts her hands on my shoulders. "Guess what! There are beautiful jocks in the world, and you're one of them!"

"It's not that, I swear," I say. "I'm just tired of soccer. Plus I have too many other things to do."

"I don't believe you," Laura says, practically sneering at me.

I get annoyed. "I don't care if you believe me or not."

"But we're a team," Rachel says, practically begging. "You can't turn your back on people who need you!"

Before I can answer, I hear Laura mutter under her breath.

"Why not? She's done it before."

LAURA

I had a feeling Calista would quit soccer eventually. I expected it. I waited for it. But now that's it happened, I can't believe it.

"You guys don't understand," Calista says, lamely. "I don't blame you for being mad, but you just don't get it."

"What don't we get?" I say, trying not to sound hurt. "That pretty girls don't play soccer? I heard Ellie and Ella yesterday. And why are you even friends with them, anyway? They were laughing today when you came down with that rash, and how about when they were too busy to even walk you to the nurse's office? They're the ones you're trying to impress?"

"Easy, Laura," Rachel says, but it's too late—the damage is done.

Calista flushes, her hives turning purple in the harsh light of the dressing room. "No! That's not it at all. I just don't want to get injured. You tackled me hard yesterday in practice and I'm lucky I didn't hurt my knee really badly and it made me scared. I don't want to spend the next six months on crutches."

"That makes sense," I say, sarcastically. "Maybe you should take up checkers, it's a lot less dangerous." I fold the dress I'm buying, then pick up my backpack and open the door to the dressing room. "Let's go, Rachel."

I start to go, but Calista calls after me. "Still friends, right?"

I just look at her. "Remember what I said before—that's what friends are for? I take it back."

We leave her standing there, and as we walk away I start to cry, which makes Rachel crazy.

"You are getting way too upset about this," she says. "It's not life or death! It's just soccer! Go let Calista live her own life, with her own friends—it's much simpler that way."

"Simpler how?" I say. "What do you mean? Because she's beautiful and I'm not, I shouldn't be able to have a friend like that?"

"No, no, no, the opposite," Rachel says. "You're like, too good for her. Way too good! And life's too short for all this drama!"

Rachel does a twirl and starts singing again. I'm amazed at her ability to be in a good mood all the time.

Why can't I be like that? "Very funny," I say. "I'm not too good for her. And she's not too pretty for me. We're two people, just like everybody else."

Rachel looks at me as if I'm three years old.

"You are so adorable," she says.

CALISTA

When I find my mom by the store entrance, she can tell right away that I'm upset.

"What's wrong?"

"Nothing. Can we just go to the car?"

"I have to pay for the dress."

"I don't want the dress!" I catch my breath. "I'm not going to the dance."

My mom grabs my hand, and we stop walking.

"What happened in there? Did you get into a fight with Laura?"

"No," I say. A few seconds later, I add, "A little." Then, a few seconds after that, I add, "I told her I'm thinking of quitting soccer."

"What? Why?"

I feel my rash get hot. "Because yesterday at practice everything started going wrong and I sweated so much I got a pimple and that was the beginning of everything going wrong and I hate soccer and I don't want to play anymore!"

My mom thinks for a minute, then decides not to argue with me. "We can talk about this later."

"I don't want to talk about it later! I have to stay after school tomorrow anyway so I can't go to practice and the team will just think I'm a spoiled brat. Forget it."

My mom's eyes went wide. "What do you mean, stay after school?"

"My English teacher hates me," I throw in, because I may as well get everything over with at once.

"Wait, what?" says my mom. "That's absurd. He doesn't even know you."

"Well, I didn't do the summer reading, and he hates me."

My mom lets out a big sigh, "Okay, slow down. I get it. It's been a long day. Let's just go home, we'll eat some dinner, you can have a nice relaxing night and start fresh tomorrow."

I nod, and we walk to the parking lot. Just as the stress starts to leave my body, my mom pauses before unlocking the door. She looks up at me.

"Okay, just so I have this straight. Two things you really used to enjoy were soccer and reading. Now you don't want to do either?"

I sniffle, more for pity than out of necessity. "Something like that, I guess."

My mom shakes her head. "I swear, I wish I knew what was going on inside that beautiful head of yours, Calista."

Then she unlocks the car and we get in.

I turn the volume way up on the radio, so it's too loud to think.

WEDNESDAY

DAMIAN

I have a morning routine.

I shower. I dress. I eat a bowl of raisin bran. I take my medication. I stuff two extra shirts into my backpack. I say goodbye to my mom and my sister. I walk to the bus stop. I get on the bus and try to sit as far away from Will Hanson as possible. It's not far enough. I ignore him and his stupid comments.

Today, though, something changes. On the bus, Patrick Toole tells Will to quit annoying me and decides to sit near me himself.

"Hey."

I nod. "Hey."

"You all good?"

I stare straight ahead. "Are you here to make stupid jokes about me, like your friend? Like, how I shouldn't elbow my way into Calista's business? Or how my lunch tasted bloody delicious? Because I would rather not hear them."

"Oh, hey, no, not at all," Patrick says. I look over at him to see if he's telling the truth, but I can't tell.

"What do you want then?"

"Someone told me you're the kid who's painting the poster for the First Week Dance?"

"Yes, that's true. Mrs. Henshaw emailed me over the summer asking if I'd do it." Mrs. Henshaw teaches art, and she's my favorite teacher at the school.

"You're a really good artist, right?"

"I don't know. I guess so. Some people think I am."

Patrick points at my backpack. "Do you have any drawings in there that I can see?"

"No."

"Okay, cool." He gets up. "See you later, Damian."

"See you later." I watch him walk to the back of the bus. I try to figure out what that was about, but can't come up with anything.

It's not until first period when I realize that the conversation on the bus was the first time Patrick Toole has ever said my name.

CALISTA

I hope I'm not imagining it, but my face has improved slightly. Hardly perfect, but a little better. My rash looks less like iguana skin. The swelling around my nose has gone down to the point where I can almost see my cheekbones. And my pimple scar is healing, leaving . . . a scab.

A scab?

Eewwww.

"Scab" is one of those words that just sounds gross. Scab. Yuck.

I stare at the scab, trying to decide what to do. I touch it. It's hard and crusty. (Are you totally disgusted yet? I know. Me, too.) I remember just twenty-four hours earlier, trying to decide what to do about something on my face. That time, I made the totally wrong call.

This time, I decide to do nothing. I don't even put a bandage on it, because we all know how well that worked out.

I go downstairs and see my dad drinking coffee and my mom reading her phone. They both barely glance up at me.

"Hi, honey," says my dad.

They've obviously decided not to bring it up. So I do.

"My face looks a little better today," I tell them.

This gives my dad permission to peek. "Wow," he says. "Looks great."

"Don't touch that scab, Calista," says my mom. "I mean it."

She looks at me but doesn't say anything else. We'd decided last night that we wouldn't talk about the soccer situation until after school. My mom wanted to give me a day to think about it.

Corey walks in, checks out my face, and scowls. "Move," he says. "I'm trying to get the cereal."

"Nice to see you, too," I tell him, which he answers by sticking his tongue out at me.

I smile. If my brother is being his usual annoying self, I know things must be heading in the right direction.

LAURA

I'm getting off the school bus when I see Calista.

"Hey, Laura," she says, smiling. She's trying to act as if nothing's changed, which is funny, since everything has.

"Are you still thinking about quitting soccer?" I ask, not letting her off the hook. "What did your mom say? Was she fine with it?"

Calista's smile fades, and I notice a thin red scab across the bridge of her nose. No bandage today. Her face is less swollen, and her rash looks a little better, too.

"I'm talking about it with my parents tonight," she says.

I decide to let it go. "Well, I hope you change your mind."

Ellie and Ella come bouncing down the hall, and I brace myself. But either they don't see us, or they pretend not to see us, because they walk right on by.

"You guys!" Calista calls to them.

They turn back, and their eyes widen like they each just saw a ghost—and not the friendly kind.

"Oh, hey," Ellie says.

"We didn't see you guys," Ella says.

Calista tries to stay cool. "Well, we're standing right here."

"Right!" Ellie laughs. "We must have been in our own heads!"

We all stand there for a few seconds, then Ellie says, "So, Calista, how's your face and stuff?"

"Yeah," Ella says, looking concerned. "Are you feeling better?" She narrows her eyes in examination. "It looks like it still really hurts."

"Actually, it's a little better," Calista says. "Thanks for asking."

"Okay, cool!" Ellie says. "Well, see you later."

"Um, actually, can you guys wait a second?" Calista says. Ellie and Ella turn back. Part of me thinks I really shouldn't be standing here listening to this, but most of me wouldn't miss it for the world.

"Yesterday," Calista says. "It was weird, right? I mean, the Patrick thing was weird, right?"

"What Patrick thing?" Ella says, blinking.

"At lunch," Calista says. I can tell how difficult this conversation is for her by how hard she's breathing. "I mean, is it really possible that he didn't ask me to the dance because I got a pimple and a rash on my face? Did that really happen?"

Ellie fidgets from one foot to the other. "I guess so. Boys can be super superficial, don't forget that."

"But here's the strange part," Calista says, her eyes narrowing. "He said he heard that I didn't want to go anyway. Do either of you guys know where he got that idea?"

Ellie and Ella look at each other.

"Um, no," Ellie says.

"Not really," Ella adds.

"I'm pretty sure one of you told him that," Calista says. "You were talking to him before I got there, remember?"

"That's crazy!" Ellie says.

"Totally insane!" Ella adds.

Calista isn't about to give in. "It would be better if you just admitted it."

Ellie's eyes flash. "Fine! It's possible I may have mentioned that I would never go to a dance if my face looked liked that. And he might have taken it the wrong way and assumed you weren't going. I can't help it if boys are dumb!"

"You guys are so lame, seriously," Calista sneers. "Come on Laura, let's go."

Before we can go anywhere, though, Ellie grabs Calista's shoulder and turns her back.

"Stop freaking out because for once in your life you didn't get something you wanted!" blurts out Ellie. "Guess what? This morning Patrick texted and asked *me* to the dance! And guess what again? I said yes!"

And just like that, the whole hallway seems to stop moving.

CALISTA

I feel my rash start to tingle.

"That's great," I tell Ellie. "No, seriously, I really think that's great." For some reason, I feel more relaxed than I have all week. It all becomes incredibly clear.

"I don't care," I add, and I mean it. "I cannot believe I have been wasting the last three days of my life worrying about some stupid dance where we all stand around staring at each other and making snarky comments about what other people are wearing and who looks good and who looks bad." I glance over at Laura. "I mean, that's crazy, right?"

I've clearly caught Laura off guard. "Um . . ." she says. "I—I mean, I guess. I was kind of looking forward to the dance, though. I mean—yeah, okay, if you want."

I suddenly lose patience with her. "Was that even English?"

"What is wrong with you?" Laura snaps back, wounded.

Ellie and Ella look at each other and giggle. As usual, my two "best friends" are bringing out the worst in me.

"Listen, Calista," Ellie says, the way a mother might talk to a sulking child. "I get that it's been a rough couple of days for you, I really do. Everyone does. Especially since you're like, the most beautiful girl ever."

"You've never had to worry about things like what to wear, how to do your hair, or what you could eat—" Ella chimes in.

"Or how popular you were," continues Ellie.

"Right, or how popular you were," echoes Ella.

"It's not like that," I protest, even though it's exactly like that.

"We still totally want to be best friends, we really do," Ellie says, sweetly. "It just seems like we should be more, like, equal best friends, instead of you being in charge all the time."

I surprise myself by grabbing Laura's arm. "Let's go, Laura," I say, but she doesn't move. I start to panic. I think about all the lousy things I've said to her over the last twelve hours—including about twenty seconds ago—and for a panicky second I feel like she's going to abandon me, too. But she nods.

"Okay, Callie," she says, and we walk away.

I guess being friends for life counts for something.

LAURA

"I'm sorry for snapping at you," Calista says to me, once we're safely down the hall. "I'm a jerk."

I shrug. "Hey, I said a few jerky things myself at the mall yesterday. It happens. Are you okay?"

"I'm great, actually," she answers. "I'm so done with those guys. I always knew they were just using me anyway."

"I always wondered why you became such good friends with them," I say. I almost add "instead of me," but don't.

Calista shakes her head. "I don't know," she says. "It just sort of happened. Like I didn't even have a choice."

"Well, girls like that tend to get what they want." We stop at our lockers. "Don't take what they say too seriously, though. Trust me—they're still in awe of you."

Calista shakes her head. "They were in awe of my looks, maybe. My hair. Not me. They couldn't care less about me."

I stare at my friend, shocked to hear these words coming out of her mouth. This was the most confident, together girl I'd ever met, two days ago. Now here she is, proving that she's just as much of a mess as the rest of us.

"I still think you should go to the dance, though," I tell her.

"Are you serious? Why?"

"Because it will mean that you can still have fun even if you're not with the cutest guy. You can prove that you're just like everybody else."

Calista thinks about that for a second. "You're right. I should go."

I smile to myself, thinking I've really gotten through to my old friend. Then she touches her scab.

"As long as my face is back to normal," she adds.

CALISTA

"Fish sticks! Gross!"

"No, I didn't see it. Was it good?"

"That homework was a joke. It was, like, totally impossible."

"I never said I didn't like that top. I love that top."

"So don't get them! Who cares? Don't make me feel bad for liking fried food! Stop talking about it."

I'm standing in line at lunch, listening to kids chattering all around me. They're talking about nothing. I want to be a part of it.

After I get a sandwich, I head out into the cafeteria. I feel like I've never seen it before, because in a way, I haven't. Normally, I would head straight for my usual table. Today, I look everywhere except my usual table.

I hear someone calling my name. "Calista! Calista! Cal!" I think it's Camille, but I don't look.

Except I do look, a little.

Out of the corner of my eye I see Ellie and Ella, waving at me to come over. Just like yesterday, Ellie is at the head of the table, in my seat. Unlike yesterday, she doesn't seem to have any intention of moving.

Eventually, I turn my head and wave. "Hey, you guys!" Very chipper, very friendly. I keep walking.

"Don't be mad! Where are you going?" says Ellie.

"Calista, are you like serious right now?" asks Ella.

I shrug and smile, then look around for any empty seat at any table of girls. I spot one and plop down.

I look up and see three faces staring at me. One girl's mouth is actually hanging open.

"Hey, you guys," I offer.

No one says hey back.

"I'm Calista."

"We know," says one girl, with short hair and blue glasses. "Are you lost?" The other girls titter.

I laugh. "Ha! No, I'm not lost. In fact, I'm exactly where I want to be."

"Okay," says a different girl, who has three earrings in her left ear. "If you say so."

As I start eating, the girls go back to their lunches and conversation. They're talking about the new drama teacher, Mr. Cassano. From what I can gather, two of the girls think he's adorable, and the other one thinks he's full of himself.

After a few minutes, I decide to join in. "Any of you

guys have Mr. Cody for English? He's really funny. Kind of strict, but funny."

The girl with the earrings stops talking and looks at me. "I'm in your class," she says.

"I was in your English class last year," says a girl with a purple streak in her hair.

"Oh yeah, totally," I say, desperately trying to place her. "Jessica, right?"

"Beth."

"Right! Beth. Sorry."

"It's okay," Beth says, and they all resume their conversation. I notice that no one is even looking at me, much less including me. I decide to try again.

"Did you guys do the summer reading?"

A few of them half nod. After a few more minutes, I feel my skin start to get hot.

"Why are you guys all ignoring me?" I ask, pretty loudly. The girls all stop talking. A strange expression comes over some of their faces, which I eventually realize is pity.

"We're not ignoring you," says the girl with the earrings. She has friendly eyes. "We just didn't think you were interested in anything we had to say."

"That's totally not true," I insist. "I'm really interested."

"What are you doing at our table?" says the blue glasses girl. "Are you in a fight with your friends?"

"It's a long, boring story."

"Does it have something to do with getting smacked in the nose?" asks Beth, pointing at my face.

"A little," I say. "Okay, a lot."

Beth smiles. "That sounds like the opposite of boring."

"I'm Shelby," says the girl with the blue glasses.

"And I'm Kara," says the girl with the earrings.

"We want to hear how you got beat up," says Beth.

"And don't leave out any of the good parts," adds Kara.

So I tell them everything.

And it feels good.

DAMIAN

After lunch, I'm on my way to Science when I pass Laura and another girl.

"Damian!" she says. "How are you? This is my friend Rachel."

"Hi, Damian, nice to meet you," says Rachel, shaking my hand. Her face changes when she feels my wet palm. "Are you okay? You're sweating."

"I'm fine, thanks. Nice to meet you."

Laura touches my hand. "Oh, you are sweating!"

I pull it away. "I sweat sometimes."

"Can I ask you something?" Laura says.

"Okay."

She points at my jacket. "Is it possible that you would sweat less if you didn't wear that thing?"

I stare down at the jacket, which I've been wearing every day for three years. It's too small now, and it's more brown than red. I don't think it smells all that great, either. But I don't want to give it up. I can't give it up.

"I like this jacket," I say.

"I know what you mean," Laura tells me. "I have this old sweatshirt that I still wear all the time, drives my parents crazy."

"I love that sweatshirt!" cries her friend Rachel.

"I know, right?" says Laura. The bell rings, which means we need to be in class in two minutes. Laura turns to me. "Well, see you later, Damian."

"Nice to meet you!" says Rachel.

They start to go, but for some reason I call after them. "I might get a new jacket soon, though."

They turn back. "As long as it says RENEGADES on it," Laura says. "I love renegades."

They walk away, and I go into the Science classroom.

"Why are you in such a good mood?" asks the teacher, Ms. Hendrickson.

"Who says I'm in such a good mood?"

She laughs. "Well, you're whistling," she says. "That's usually a telltale sign."

"Huh," I say. I had no idea I was whistling.

I had no idea I even knew how to whistle, to tell you the truth.

LAURA

"Where's Calista?" barks Coach Sweeney.

Everyone on the team stares at the grass.

"Where's Getz?" she barks again, louder. "Anyone?"

Girls' heads veer in my direction, as if I know the answer. Which I do.

"Uh, she had to stay after school today."

Giggles all around.

Coach frowns. "Stay after school? For what? She get in trouble?"

"Not exactly," I say. "She just—she didn't do her summer reading assignment. Everyone who didn't do it has to go to after-school study hall until they finish the book."

"I see." Coach tries not to look worried. "So she'll be here tomorrow?"

I'm not sure what to say, until I come up with, "I guess it depends on whether or not she finishes the book."

"Well, she better be a darn fast reader." Coach blows her whistle for what seems like twenty deafening seconds. "Okay! Everyone on the field for stretches! Double time, let's go!"

We practice hard for ninety minutes. At one point, my teammate Danielle is flying down the left wing with the ball, and I think she's about to sprint past me, but at the last minute I make a clean tackle and strip the ball away. Then I feed Brianna streaking down the right sideline, and she scores.

"Calista Getz who?" Rachel yells, as I run back on defense. "That was awesome!"

We high-five. "Yeah, who needs her?" I say, and we both laugh.

That's the closest anyone comes to getting by me all day. I totally dominate the rest of the scrimmage.

It feels awesome.

And a tiny bit boring.

CALISTA

Mr. Cody welcomes me like a long lost friend.
"Calista! So good to see you! Grab a seat anywhere, as long as it's not right next to someone else. We're not looking for any distractions."

I look around the room. I see Will Hanson, slouched down, holding his book like it's a dead rat. I recognize two other kids, Chris and Janelle, but there are four others whose names I don't know. I remember lunch, and it slowly dawns on me that there are a lot of kids in school I don't know by name, and have never even spoken to. I feel a weird sense of shame about that for a second, before Mr. Cody jolts me back to reality.

"Ms. Getz? A seat?"

"Oh, sorry . . . right."

I find a seat in the back row and plop down.

"Let's get cracking, shall we? No time like the present!"

Mr. Cody takes out a book of his own and sits behind the desk. I open mine and start reading.

It turns out to be really good.

It's interesting, and the story is intense, and I care about the characters, and I can't wait to find out what happens next, and—

"Okay, time," announces a voice.

Wait, what?

I raise my hand. "What do you mean, time?"

"I mean, that's forty minutes," says Mr. Cody. "Study hall is over. You're free to leave."

I look at the clock. He's right. Forty minutes have gone by. It seemed like five. Actually, it seemed like none.

"This book isn't terrible," offers Will Hanson.

"I'll be sure to tell the author you said so," says Mr. Cody.

Will snorts as he gets up. "Later, peeps."

Mr. Cody shakes his head. "Peeps? Really?"

I start gathering up my stuff, and Mr. Cody comes over to my desk. "You're enjoying it?"

"Yeah, it's really good."

"That's great." He takes a seat at the desk next to me. "So how's that nose of yours?"

"Fine, I guess. Still hurts a little."

"It does look like it's getting better." Mr. Cody claps his hands together. "Anyway, that's enough learning for today. I received a text from my colleague Coach Sweeney a few minutes ago, she said that you're running late for practice. You better get going! No contact drills, though. See you tomorrow."

"Actually, I'm not sure I'm playing soccer this year," I say. I have no idea why I tell him that, but there it is. Now I'm going to have to hear all about what a bad decision that is, how sports build character, blah blah blah—

"I think that's an excellent idea," Mr. Cody says.

Huh?

"You do?"

"I totally do."

"Oh. I thought you were going to say something different."

"Nope." Mr. Cody sits back behind his desk. "Couldn't agree more. Girls shouldn't play sports."

I stop in my tracks.

"Excuse me?"

"Girls shouldn't play sports," he repeats.

"Are you kidding?" I repeat, as my heart starts to beat a little faster. "Why not?" I'm not sure what I'm feeling at first, then I recognize it. Anger.

"Think of all the stuff you guys have to deal with these days," Mr. Cody says, and I notice he's got this quirky smile on his face as he says it. "Nails, hair, makeup. Making sure you look pretty. Why would you want to mess that up?" He points at my face. "Plus, you get injuries like that nose of yours. Not very lady-like."

"That's not how that happened," I say sharply. "It happened at lunch. I thought you knew that."

"Oh, right," he says, holding up his hands. "I forgot. Sorry. Why are you annoyed? I'm agreeing with your decision."

"I have to go," I tell him.

"Okay, see you tomorrow," he says, and goes back to his reading.

I pick up my backpack, then immediately put it back down. "Why would I be annoyed because of some crazy theory of yours? You better hope I don't tell people what you said, by the way. You could get in trouble."

Mr. Cody puts his book down. "I know I could. But isn't that exactly what this is about?"

"What do you mean?"

"You know what I mean," he says, and I suddenly realize he's been sarcastic this whole time.

"Oh," I say. "I get it."

He gives a little laugh and shakes his head. "It's sad that there are actually people who think like that. But remember, it's always up to you. If you like soccer, play soccer! Don't listen to anyone else. Make up your own mind."

"I gotta go." I sling my backpack over my shoulder

and walk down the hall without looking back. But when I turn the corner, I stop and lean against the locker.

Make up your own mind.

Easier said than done.

DAMIAN

Mrs. Henshaw, the art teacher, is cleaning the paint brushes when I walk into her studio after school.

"Mr. White!" she sings, when she sees me. She's one of those people who is always in a good mood. I kind of wish I was like that.

"Hey, Mrs. Henshaw." I pull out my sketch pad.

"Oh, you won't be using that," she says. Then she points at the giant easel in the middle of the room. "This is a big poster, for the school dance! You're going to be painting giant, swooping, moving figures that catch our school spirit for all to see!"

"Okay," I say. I'm nervous. I've never worked on such a big canvas before. "Uh, but don't I need people to draw? I'm not the type of person who can just sketch someone out of thin air—"

"Taken care of!" Mrs. Henshaw chirps, opening up the door to her inner office. Out walks Patrick Toole.

"Hey," he says.

"What are you doing here?" I ask.

He laughs. "Getting extra credit, dude, what do you think I'm doing?"

"Meet your model," Mrs. Henshaw says, grinning.

"He's my model?" I look at Patrick, shocked. "So, wait. Is that why you were asking me all those questions on the bus?"

"Yeah, maybe." He sits on one of the stools in the art room. Actually, it's more of a slouch. I wish I could slouch like that.

"So what do I have to do?" Patrick asks.

"Be a good boy and stay still," says Mrs. Henshaw. "Can you do that?"

Patrick shrugs. "How hard can it be?"

Mrs. Henshaw laughs. "Pretty hard, actually,"

"You probably don't need extra credit," Patrick says to me. "You're an art guy. I'm not an art guy at all."

"Can you dance?" I ask him.

"Can I dance? Why?"

"Because I need you to strike a dance pose."

"Are you serious?" Patrick rolls his eyes and looks at Mrs. Henshaw. "You didn't say anything about striking some pose."

"Oh, relax, you," she says to him. "It's no big deal. And you will be the star of the school!"

Patrick grumbles under his breath, but gets out of his chair. "Pose like how?"

Mrs. Henshaw puts Patrick's arms in the air and

sticks his legs out at funny angles, as if he's a piece of clay. Patrick tries to be still, but keeps shifting around. It turns out Mrs. Henshaw was right—posing is hard.

Finally Patrick manages to keep still, but we're missing something pretty obvious. "Who's the girl model?" I ask Mrs. Henshaw.

She smacks herself on the forehead and starts to pace. "Oh, no!" she mutters, mostly to herself. "I knew I forgot something! How could I be so foolish?"

I put my brush down. "What are we going to do?"

Just then, Calista Getz walks by.

CALISTA

Walking down the hall, I decide to text my mom.

AFTER-SCHOOL READING IS OVER. CAN YOU PICK ME UP IN TEN MINUTES?

TWENTY, she texts back. JUST FINISHING UP WITH CLIENT.

OKAY. DO I HAVE DANCE CLASS TONIGHT?

YES 6:30.

I put my phone away and start heading toward the front doors when I hear voices coming from the art room. I walk over and see Damian White, in his red jacket of course. He's talking to someone I can't see.

Before I can decide whether or not I want to say hi, Mrs. Henshaw's voice rings out down the hall.

"Calista! Calista dear!"

I smile and wave weakly. "Hey."

Grabbing my hand, she pulls me into the room. "You're just in time!"

"Just in time for what?"

That's when I notice Patrick Toole, standing there with his arms and legs spread out like he's striking some sort of crazy yoga pose.

Even though I'm not exactly a huge Patrick Toole fan at the moment, I can't help but laugh out loud. It feels like the first time I've really laughed in three days.

"Holy moly," I say. "You look ridiculous."

"That's really not helpful," Patrick says.

"Well, sorry, but it's true."

"I guess." He shrugs, then looks away. Neither one of us knows what to say next. The memory of our last conversation is still in my head. It's probably in his head, too.

"Well, see you later," I say, starting to walk away.

"Patrick needs a partner," Mrs. Henshaw says. "Are you available?"

I stop. "A partner for what?"

Patrick moves his head slightly my way. "Damian is making the poster for the First Week Dance," he says. "It's supposed to be a couple dancing, but so far there's just me. You could be the girl. You can get extra credit."

I shake my head. "Why not ask Ellie? You're going to the dance with her, after all."

Patrick blushes and looks down, then back at me. "Mrs. Henshaw asked *you*."

I immediately touch my face. The skin feels warm

where the rash is. I realize I haven't looked in the mirror in a few hours. I don't know what I look like.

"I don't think so," I say. Then to Damian, I say, "Why would you want me to pose?"

"What do you mean?" Damian asks.

"You know . . . with my face."

"Your face looks fine," says Patrick, still trying not to move. "I mean, yeah, it's not what you usually look like, but I'm sure Damian will make you look perfect, right Damian?"

"Right," Damian says.

Patrick scratches his knee, then puts his arm back in place. "So, can we get on with it? I'm dying up here."

"Calista, dear?" says Mrs. Henshaw. "Shall we?"

"How about this?" I say. "I can pose and you can use everything except my face. You have to use somebody else's face, like a model from a book or something. Is that fair?"

I can tell by Damian's expression that he thinks I'm being weird, but he nods. "Okay. Can you start now?"

I shake my head. "I can't. My mom is coming to pick me up, and I have dance class in an hour. I could come tomorrow after school, maybe."

"You're a dancer?" Mrs. Henshaw says, clapping her hands together. "Even better!"

"Whoa," moans Patrick. "I'm going to have to come back tomorrow and do this all over again?"

"Is that so horrible?" Mrs. Henshaw says.

Patrick shrugs. "I guess not." Then he looks at me. "As long as you make Calista look just as ridiculous as me," he says, grinning.

I try not to smile back, but do anyway. "I gotta go."

On my way outside, I take out my phone and start texting Ellie and Ella. It's like a reflex, but when I realize what I'm doing I stop. I put my phone away, pull out my book, and start reading.

The first time my mom honks, I don't even hear her.

DAMIAN

I sketch Patrick for about ten more minutes before we both decide to just start over the next day when Calista joins us.

"Again, I apologize," says Mrs. Henshaw. "This was my fault. I totally forgot about the girl! I must be getting old."

"You're not old," I tell her. "You're just an artist, and artists are forgetful sometimes."

"You're such a dear," Mrs. Henshaw says, patting my back.

"Are you forgetful?" Patrick asks me.

"I don't know," I say. "Why?"

"Well, you're an artist."

"I am?" I smile. Patrick calling me an artist makes me feel good.

Mrs. Henshaw disappears back into her office and Patrick and I both take out our phones. After about a minute, Patrick says, "So, you and Calista are friends?"

"A little, I guess."

"Did you know her before you bonked her in the nose?" He notices me blush and adds, "No offense or anything."

"We met when I moved here last year. And yesterday before lunch I was in the nurse's office when she came in with her rash."

"What were you in for?"

"Oh, nothing really." I rub my arms, feeling the leather of my jacket, old, cracked, rough to the touch. "I just wasn't feeling great, I think."

"Are you better now? I hope it's not contagious."

"Yeah, I'm good."

"She's a pretty interesting person," Patrick says.

"Calista?"

"Yeah."

"I guess."

"I messed up." Patrick gets up and starts pacing around the room. "I, like, totally wanted to ask her to the dance but then all this stuff started happening and my friends and her friends said I couldn't go with a girl with a rash and I convinced myself she wasn't going to go and before I knew it Will talked me into asking Ellie and now it's too late to do anything about it."

"Oh," I say.

He stops pacing and looks at me. "You think I can make it up to her? I really want to make it up to her."

"I guess." I stand up. "Just tell her the truth."

"The truth?" Patrick says. "That makes sense! Thanks, dude."

"You're welcome."

"What about you?" Patrick asks me. "Anyone you like?"

I feel a bead of sweat pop out on my arm. "What do you mean? Like, a girl?"

He laughs. "Yeah, like a girl."

"No."

"What about that girl, Laura?" Patrick asks. "That's her name, right? I saw you guys talking in the hall. Looked like it was going well."

"Yes, that's her name," I say, my heart racing a mile a minute.

"She seems cool." Patrick grins. "Maybe give it a shot? Like my football coach always says, you can't win if you don't play."

"I gotta go," I say. "My sister's picking me up."

"Whoa, hope I didn't scare you," Patrick says, smacking me on the back. "You're a good dude. And you're going to draw a cool poster, right? You won't make me look like an idiot?"

"I will not," I promise him.

"Great!" He throws his backpack over his shoulder

and runs out of the room. A few seconds later, he sticks his head back in.

"Cool jacket you got there, by the way," he says. "It's, like, so beat up and grimy! I love it."

I think about telling him that Laura said I needed a new one, but I decide not to.

CALISTA

I've been dancing since before I can remember. It feels as natural to me now as breathing. It helps me forget about the rest of the world.

Also, I'm not very good at it.

So I don't feel any pressure when I go to dance class: it's just a way to relax and have fun.

It's nice to be one of the many, instead of one of the few.

The instructor, Cindy, used to dance on Broadway, which is something I can't even conceive of. It's like being from another planet or something.

When she sees me come in, she runs over and gives me a big hug, since it's the first class after summer break. "Calista! You've grown like a weed!" Then she notices my face, and smiles. "What happened to you?"

I stare at her in shock. "Sorry?"

"Your face. What happened to it?" Cindy repeats.

"You look like you got hit by a truck. And I see you got a pimple, huh? Your first one?"

"How could you tell?" I mumble, mortified.

Cindy laughs. "People always pick the first one, even if it's in the worst place, and I recognize a picked-pimple-scab when I see one. Youch."

After a second, I realize that she's the first person in three days to actually tell me that I look terrible. It makes me feel different. It makes me feel relaxed.

"Yup, I picked it," I tell her. "Also, I put some of my mom's concealer on it and I had an allergic reaction, which is where the rash came from. And then my nose—well, that happened at school and it's too complicated to explain."

"Very cool!" Cindy says. "Sounds like you've been through the wringer a little bit. It's all good, though—builds character. And that first zit is like a badge of honor." She suddenly gives me a big hug. "Welcome to the sisterhood."

"Okay," I say. "Uh, what does that mean?"

"It means, it's not the end of the world," Cindy says. "It's not the end of anything. In fact, it might be the beginning of everything." She claps her hands together. "Okay everybody, let's do this!"

We all spread out around the room and start our stretches. For the next hour and a half, I do nothing but dance. I stumble and bumble, I trip and almost wipe out,

I fall behind the beat about fifty times, I feel my muscles yelling at me in protest.

It feels great.

THURSDAY

LAURA

I wake up to a text from Calista: CAN WE TALK? I HAVE AN IDEA

I wait a few minutes before texting back.

SURE.

DAMIAN

Before leaving for school, I stare at my red jacket for about five minutes before deciding to put it on.

On the bus, Patrick waves but walks by me without saying anything. I wave back.

After five minutes, Will comes over and takes his usual seat across the aisle from me, but before he can say anything, I say, "Not today."

He looks shocked. "Did you just say 'not today'?"

"Yes. Not today."

"Whoa," Will says. "Look who's feeling all brave."

"Just leave me alone."

Will looks as if he wants to say about a thousand things. But he doesn't say any of them. Instead, he mutters, "Sweatbox," and walks away. I pretend not to hear him.

I take out my pad and start sketching. Three minutes later I hear a voice behind me saying, "That's pretty good. What is it?"

I turn around to see Patrick sitting there. I had no idea he was right behind me.

"A sand dune," I tell him. "Somewhere in the desert."

"You can almost feel the heat," he says.

I smile inside. "Really?"

"Kind of," Patrick says, laughing. "Mostly I just thought it sounded good. You like drawing deserts?"

"I guess so."

"That's cool. A little weird, but cool. See you after school."

"Okay."

I go back to my drawing.

I tell myself that this is going to be the last desert I draw for a while.

Maybe ever.

CALISTA

Who is that?

Believe it or not, that's the first thought that pops into my head when I look at myself in the mirror. It's my face, my almost-regular face, but I feel like I'm looking at a stranger.

I can start to see the real me in there, but it's almost like the person who had that face isn't who I am anymore.

I trace my finger along the small scab that's formed on my nose. I rub my cheeks and my neck, which still have a few blotchy spots, if you really look for them. I touch my nose, which is still a little tender, still a little swollen, but definitely within human proportions.

I smile to myself. I feel relieved. I feel better. I feel almost happy.

But mainly, I feel different.

LAURA

In homeroom, Ellie and Ella wave as soon as they see me.

"Laura! Laura!"

Oh, wonderful.

I sigh and walk over.

"Did you pick out a dress for tomorrow night?" That's Ellie.

"Are you excited?" That's Ella.

"I'm pretty excited," I say, unexcitedly. "How about you guys?"

"Can't wait!" That's both of them.

"Awesome," I say, turning to go. But Ellie grabs my arm.

"Is Calista mad at us?"

"Oh, I don't know," I say. "Why would she be mad at you guys? Just because you dropped her like a hot potato when she had a rough few days, then went behind her back and convinced the guy she likes to not ask her to the dance, but to ask you instead?" I laugh sarcastically. "Not to mention the fact that you were both too busy to bring her backpack to the nurse's office when she practically broke her nose? Who would be mad at that? That's crazy."

"That's not how it happened," Ellie sniffs.

"That's not how it happened at all," Ella adds, in case I missed it the first time.

"Whatever. I need to go sit down now."

I head to my seat, feeling pretty good about things, when I see Calista walk in. I go up to her.

"I got your text. You wanted to talk?"

"I did." Calista looks around the room, and then pulls me into a corner. "I have a question for you: Do you have a date to the dance?"

I blink. "Huh? Uh, no. Why?"

"I think I have someone for you."

I have been friends with Calista for six years, and never once have we talked about boys. She's always had other friends for that. I wish I didn't care, but I do.

I can feel my heart beat faster. "Really? Who?"

Her gaze shifts over to the left, and she nods her head, just a tiny bit. I follow her eyes right to the front row, third desk in.

"Damian?" I say. "Why Damian?"

"He's really nice," Calista says.

"How do you know?"

"We're friends."

"Really?" I have a hard time believing that someone like Calista could be friends with someone like Damian. I know that makes me sound like a terrible person, but hey—I'm just being honest.

"Wait a second—did you guys bond when he punched you in the nose?" I ask. "Jeez, I gotta try that sometime."

"Haha," Calista says. "You know that was an accident. So, should I tell him to ask you?"

"Wait a second," I say, feeling a little offended. "It kind of feels like you're trying to do me some sort of favor. How would you know if he even likes me?"

"I don't. I'm just saying, give it a chance. We've had a few conversations and he just seems pretty cool, that's all. So how about it?"

I start to get annoyed at Calista's pushiness. "If he's so cool, why don't you go with him?"

"I don't know," she says. "I guess maybe because he seems more like your type."

"Why's that? Because he's a little weird and a little weird-looking?"

Calista's eyes widen in protest. "Not at all!"

By now, my insecurity is kicking into overdrive. "I'm not your pet project, Callie, and he's not a charity case. To be honest, it's a little demeaning that you would assume I would want to go to the dance with some gawky guy I barely know."

Calista shrinks back a few steps, like I actually

physically pushed her. "Wow. You know something? You're no better than Ellie and Ella. You can't see beyond what Damian looks like, or seems like, to actually consider the fact that he might be an awesome guy. Sorry, I didn't realize you were too good for him."

"I never said that!"

"Well, it sure felt like it." Calista's face is getting red, and I see a few splotches around her neck and cheeks where her rash is still hanging on. "Just forget it."

"I will."

We both take our seats. A few seconds later, I hear giggling and I turn around. Ella and Ellie are sitting there, waving at me.

"Poor baby get her feelings hurt?" says Ella, and they both crack up.

"Mind your own business," I tell them, but the most aggravating thing is, they're right.

That's exactly what happened.

CALISTA

I sit at my desk, trying to calm myself down, but it doesn't work. I can't figure people out. I thought I was doing a nice thing. The last thing I would do is try to hurt Laura's feelings.

I see a bunch of hands go up around the room, and I realize Ms. Harnick must have just asked a question.

"What about you, Calista?"

I sit, frozen.

"Do you want me to put you down for set-up or clean-up tomorrow night?"

"Yes."

The class giggles.

"Sorry?" Ms. Harnick says. "For the dance? Set-up or clean-up?"

"Oh. Sorry. Um, set-up, I guess."

"Terrific," says Ms. Harnick.

The bell rings, and we all head off to our first class.

Laura brushes by me without saying anything. Ellie and Ella don't even look at me. People are whirling by all around me, and I feel invisible, until finally I hear, "Calista! How's it going?"

I turn around and see a girl standing there with short hair and blue glasses. I panic for a second, not remembering her name, but then it comes to me. "Shelby! Hi! Nice to see you!"

"You, too," says Shelby. She stands there for a second, then adds, "Are you okay? You seem a little frazzled."

"Yeah, no, I'm fine. Just a little—some stuff on my mind, that's all."

Shelby nods. "We can talk about it at lunch, if you want."

"That'd be great."

"Cool. See you later."

Shelby smiles and walks away.

I feel a little better.

Amazing what a ten-second conversation can do.

DAMIAN

Mr. Decker blows the whistle, and the game begins.

We're playing three-on-three again, and as usual, I'm the tallest one on the court. I score two quick baskets against Will Hanson, who's guarding me. Then I block Will's shot and grab the rebound.

"Let me take him," growls Patrick, pushing Will out of the way.

I pass the ball to Jeffrey, who's on my team. Jeffrey catches it like it's covered with snakes, then quickly throws it back to me, except he throws it at my feet. The ball bounces off my shins; Patrick grabs it and scores an easy basket.

"Good try, Jeffrey," I say. "Just pass it back to me nice and easy."

"I would if I could," Jeffrey whines. I know what he means. I was scared of basketball, too, until a few years ago, when my growth spurt made it much easier.

The third kid on our team, Steven, tosses the ball in-bounds to Jeffrey. He quickly throws it to me, and this time I catch it. I back down the lane, with Patrick furiously swiping at the ball. He's quick and strong, but I'm about three inches taller than him. I pick up my dribble and hold the ball high, where he can't come close to reaching it. Then I fake a shot, and he jumps high in the air. I wait until he goes by, then put in a lay-up.

"Game!" hollers Mr. Decker. "Two-minute break!" We only play to three, so everyone gets a chance to rotate in and out quickly.

I run to the sidelines. Patrick comes over and smacks me in the back. "Good game," he says. "You should think about coming out for travel. You've got a sweet touch for a tall guy."

"Thanks," I say. "I don't know."

"I'm serious, dude."

"Okay. I'll think about it."

Will walks by and grunts, "Not bad," on his way to the water fountain.

That's never happened before.

I look down at my shirt. It's covered with sweat. My shorts are damp. I walk over to the sideline to grab the towel that I always leave under the basket.

"Nice game," a voice says. A girl's voice.

I look up and see Laura standing there. "You were watching?" I ask.

"Yup," she says. "You were beating the cocky school jocks. How could I not watch? It was awesome, by the way."

"Thanks."

"You're a really good basketball player."

"So are you."

"You've never seen me play!" she says, laughing.

"Oh, yeah."

We both laugh. Then we both stop laughing and look at each other. It's weird, in a good way. Then it starts to get weird, in an awkward way.

Mr. Decker comes over, just in the nick of time.

"Good playing today, Damian," he says. "You're starting to put your game together and show some real skill. See you tomorrow."

I don't move.

"Damian?" Coach says. "You're good for today. You got a real workout in."

"I think I'll stay."

Mr. Decker's eyes go wide with surprise. "You want to stay for the whole gym class? Are you sure?"

I nod. "Yes, I'm sure."

"Excellent!" He smacks me on the back, right where Patrick smacked me, so it actually hurts a little.

But not really.

I play six more games, and win five.

CALISTA

Mr. Decker blows the whistle, and the game begins.

We're in the middle of a one-on-one tournament, and I'm playing against Camille. I'm a little nervous, still thinking about what happened the last time I played basketball in gym—sweat, hives, nightmare. Camille scores a quick basket on me, while I miss my first four shots.

She scores another basket and looks at me. "Whoa," she says. "You look like you're playing scared."

"I'm not," I insist. But she's right, I am.

I glance down to the other end of the court, where the boys are playing three-on-three. Patrick is guarding Damian and they have a good battle going on, but Damian puts on a good move and scores. I look up at the clock, surprised to see him still playing. Usually he's at the nurse's office by now.

"You ready?" Camille says.

"Yeah."

It's 2-0. We're playing to three, so if she scores again I

lose. It's my ball. I shoot and miss. We both jump for the rebound, and the ball deflects toward the sideline. Without thinking, I dive on the floor to try and save it. The ball goes out of bounds anyway.

"You're bleeding," Camille tells me. I look down and see I've skinned my knee. It starts to hurt a little bit. It feels good.

"Do you want me to get Mr. Decker?" she asks.

"No," I say. "Let's keep playing."

I feel like a light has switched on. I start to play hard. It feels like something or someone has set me free. I beat Camille, 3-2, then beat Rachel, 3-1. After two more games, I make it to the finals of the tournament, where I play Laura. It makes sense that we're in the finals. We used to shoot baskets at her house for hours.

We eye each other warily as the game starts. The score is close. I know all her moves, so I can anticipate where she's going before she gets there. But she does the same to me. It's a defensive battle. The game lasts forever, but eventually it's 2-2. The other games are over and gym class is about to end, so the rest of the kids come over to watch—girls and boys. Laura drives, but I block her shot. The ball goes flying out of bounds, where it smacks Ellie in the shoulder.

"Ow!" she hollers. "Watch it!"

Everyone laughs, which makes her mad, which makes it even more hilarious.

Laura tries to dribble around me but I poke the ball

away, and it hits her knee before going out. My ball. I throw it to Laura to check it, she throws it back, and I immediately drive to the basket. I'm about to go up for a layup when Laura bumps me from behind. It sends me sprawling, but just before I hit the floor, I throw the ball up toward the basket. Miraculously, it goes in. Everyone gasps in disbelief.

"That's the game!" cries Mr. Decker. "One-on-one girls champion, Calista Getz!"

I glance over at the crowd and see Patrick and Damian standing next to each other, cheering.

For some reason, that makes me feel even better than the shot going in.

LAURA

You gotta be kidding me.

I stare at the ball as it flies through the air. Even though there's no possible way it should go in, I know that it will.

And it does.

The game is over. Calista wins, 3-2, which means she wins the whole tournament. My first reaction is disbelief. My second reaction is crushing disappointment. And my third reaction is, hey, wait a second. This could be a good thing.

I wait for everyone to congratulate Calista before going up to her. She is sweaty, and her face is red, and you can see the last gasps of her rash just below her chin. Her nose is slightly purple but otherwise looks normal. The scab on her nose is tiny. Her Calistian perfection is almost completely back. Order in the world has been restored.

"Good game," I say.

She nods, still breathing hard. "You, too."

"You're a somewhat decent athlete, did you know that?"

Calista laughs. "I guess so."

Mr. Decker comes up to us. "Terrific game, both of you," he says. "You're teammates on the travel soccer team, correct? The team must be pretty darn good."

I look at Calista. She looks at me. I decide to take the leap.

"We've been known to dominate a game or two," I say. "Right, Callie?"

She hesitates, then nods. "Yup," she says. "We sure have."

CALISTA

My knee is throbbing a little bit as I head to English class. I stop in to the nurse's office to see if I can get some aspirin. The first thing I see is Damian, sitting up on his usual table.

"Hey," we say to each other.

"Amazing shot," he says. "I couldn't believe that went in."

"Neither could I," I tell him. "So, uh, I noticed you stayed for the whole gym class?"

"I decided to stay."

"What about your—you know—sweating thing?"

"I think the medicine is working a little better," Damian says. "And everyone sweats when they play basketball, right?"

I laugh. "I guess so."

"Hello!" says Nurse Kline. "If it isn't my two favorite customers!"

"Yup," I say. "That's us."

It's Damian's turn to laugh.

"Not for long," he tells Nurse Kline. "Not for long."

DAMIAN

After I change my shirt and Calista gets her aspirin, we walk together to English class.

"So," she says, "I'll make you a deal."

We keep walking.

"What kind of deal?"

When we get to the door of the classroom, neither one of us makes a move to open it.

"What kind of deal?" I repeat.

"I know I agreed to pose for the poster," Calista says. "But in return, you have to agree to stay at the dance. You can't just drop your poster off and leave."

This is not something I'm used to talking about— ever—so my heart starts to pound. "Oh," I say, hopefully sounding way calmer than I actually am. "I don't usually go to dances or stuff like that."

"Well, maybe it's time."

"I'll think about it," I say.

"Don't think about it too much," Calista says. "Just come."

As we're about to go into class, she stops me for a second. "But think about losing the jacket, okay?" she says. "Just, you know—think about it."

"Fine," I say. A couple of seconds later, I add, "Okay, I thought about it. No."

She laughs. "You're funny, Damian White," she says.

I walk to my desk, thinking that one over.

I've been called a lot of things, but "funny" was never one of them.

CALISTA

Mr. Cody claps his hands together to get our attention.

"First of all, I'm looking forward to seeing all my readers again today after school."

I raise my hand.

"Sorry, but I have to go to the art room to pose for a poster. It's for the First Week Dance."

Mr. Cody frowns. "That's great, and you can certainly do that, after you spend forty minutes finishing your summer reading with your fellow students."

I raise my hand again. He looks annoyed. "What is it, Calista?"

"One more thing I forgot to say."

"And that is?"

I can't help but grin. "I finished the book."

"Well." Mr. Cody leans back on his desk. "That's a horse of a different color."

"I finished it last night," I tell him. "It was good. I really liked it."

"Well, I'm impressed. And I'm glad you liked it." He looks around the class. "Did any of the rest of you stragglers manage to pull off that miraculous feat last night?"

No hands go up.

"Okay then," Mr. Cody says. "I'll see the rest of you after school."

He looks at me. "Calista, congratulations. You're the proud owner of one get-out-of-jail-free card."

I notice Laura looking at me. "Seriously?" she whispers. "You finished the book?" she says.

"Seriously, I did," I whisper back. "Why are you so shocked? It's the new me!"

She laughs. "More like the old you."

DAMIAN

"Today's the day!" sings Mrs. Henshaw as I walk into her studio after school. "We must finish this today!"

"I will," I say. "Or tonight. Or maybe tomorrow."

"Ha!" Mrs. Henshaw says. "Aren't you the funny one all of a sudden?"

"I guess so," I answer.

I've just started taking out the brushes when Patrick walks in. "Dude," he says. It takes me a second to realize he's referring to me. "You ready to roll?"

"Uh, yeah, but we should really wait for Calista, I think."

"Oh yeah, right." Patrick sits and takes out his phone and starts playing a game. "Whoa!" he yells, then laughs. "No way!"

"What happened?" I ask.

"Oh, nothing," he says. "This game is just so totally insane." He starts playing again and cracks up at his phone. "Insane!"

Watching him makes me wish I could have fun so easily.

A few minutes later, Calista walks in. "Sorry I'm late. I was in the nurse's office."

"Why?" I ask. "Is everything okay?"

"Oh yeah, I'm fine," she says. "I just needed to grab a book I left in there."

"Cool," I say.

Calista looks at me. "Nurse Kline told me she doesn't expect to see you at all tomorrow."

"I have a really busy day," I say.

"Busy is good," Calista says.

Mrs. Henshaw comes buzzing into the room. "No more chitchat! We're here to work!"

Patrick and Calista stand up on the two apple-boxes Mrs. Henshaw has pushed together.

"How's it going?" Patrick asks Calista.

"Pretty good," she answers.

"Cool," he says. "Your face looks all better, practically."

"It's getting there."

They keep talking as they strike a dance pose. I start painting, trying not to pay attention to what they're saying.

I hear every word.

CALISTA

Mrs. Henshaw takes Patrick's hand and puts it on my waist, then she takes mine and puts it on his shoulder. She asks us to bring our other hands together in the air.

"Seriously?" asks Patrick. "No offense or anything, but isn't this how old people dance?"

"Old people, young people—anyone with class," sniffs Mrs. Henshaw. "Now you two just hush yourselves and look pretty."

We stand there and look pretty.

"Are we allowed to talk?" I ask Damian.

He nods. "Sure, as long as you don't move."

"Can we move our mouths?"

"Yes, slightly," Damian says, not taking his eyes off his canvas.

I look at Patrick. "So."

"Yeah," he says.

Our faces are approximately three inches apart. For

some reason, instead of making me shy, it makes me bold. "So," I say again. "Do you like Ellie?"

I feel Patrick's shoulder tensing up beneath my hand. "Are you serious? You really want to talk about that now? Here?"

"Why not?" I ask.

"Yes! No! Maybe!" he says. Then he adds quietly, "I like you."

"So then why did you ask her to the dance?"

He shifts his feet.

"Last I checked," I add, "you're only supposed to ask someone to the dance if you like them. Right, Damian?"

Damian blushes and doesn't look up. "Please stop moving," he says.

"Was it because," I ask Patrick, "all of a sudden, I wasn't the prettiest girl in school anymore?"

Patrick looks around like he's trapped in a bad dream. "Of course not," he mumbles. "I don't know. I'm sorry."

"You guys, stop moving!" Damian commands.

"Sorry for what?" I ask Patrick.

He tries not to fidget. "I—I messed it all up. I didn't treat you fairly."

"Well, that's true, you didn't."

"I'm really sorry," Patrick repeats, and all of a sudden I feel bad for him.

"It's okay," I say. "I'm just kidding around, anyway."

He blinks. "You are? About what?"

"The whole thing."

"Huh?"

I shrug, as if I don't have a care in the world. "People are so obsessed with looks, it's gross."

Patrick looks like he doesn't know who I am anymore. Which would make two of us. I scratch my nose for a second, then place my hand back in his and decide to change the subject. "Damian, when can we see the poster?"

He shakes his head. "Not for a while."

"Seriously?" I ask. "Why not?"

"I never show anybody my unfinished work."

"Mrs. Henshaw, is that true?" Patrick says. "We can't see the poster?"

"Damian, let them take a look at your work-in-progress," she says.

"Fine. Five minutes," Damian says.

"How much longer do we have to pose?" Patrick asks.

"Five minutes," Damian says again.

Patrick chuckles. "Is five minutes your answer for everything?"

"Damian, what's two minutes plus two minutes?" I ask him.

"Four minutes," he says.

"Shush, you two!" whispers Mrs. Henshaw. "Let the man do his work."

Seven minutes later, Damian says, "Okay, you can look at it now if you want."

Patrick and I immediately jump down from the apple-boxes and rush over to the easel where Damian is working. I stare at the white canvas—all I see is a vague outline of our body shapes, in a formal dance pose.

"That's it?" I say.

"Where's the rest?" Patrick adds.

"Today I just needed to work on your body shapes," Damian says. "Tonight I'll do the faces, and I know what your faces look like. Plus I have the yearbook pictures if I need them."

"So you're going to use my face after all?" I ask him.

"I'd like to," Damian says. "Is that still a problem?"

I think for a second. I'm feeling better, and my yearbook picture looks good. "It's okay, I guess," I say. "When can we see the final product?"

"I'm going to work some more on it tonight and finish it tomorrow before the dance," Damian says.

"Well aren't you a last-minute Larry?" I say.

Mrs. Henshaw comes up to me and pinches my cheek. "Relax, you're a beautiful girl," she says, reminding me of my grandmother. "You have absolutely nothing to worry about."

"You're so nice," I say. "Thank you."

Patrick is smiling at me as he puts on his jacket. *"People are so obsessed with looks, it's gross,"* he says, imitating me.

"Watch it," I tell him.

"Oh, I will," he says.

DAMIAN

After dinner, I wait until my mom and my sister go in to watch TV, then I take out the poster. I don't have an easel at home so I spread a bunch of newspapers out on the dining room table, then put the poster down over that. I bring over a lamp so I can see better.

I take out my paint brushes.

I stare at the two dancing bodies, then start to fill them in—the colors, the shadows, the depth, the perspective. It takes me a while, until finally I'm satisfied. But I'm not done yet, of course.

I still have to do the faces.

I paint Patrick first. I have the yearbook open to his picture, and it goes quickly. He's got an easy face to paint. Not complicated.

Calista is different. Harder. I put the paintbrush down and look at her yearbook picture for a long time, but it doesn't help that much. She doesn't look real in that picture, she doesn't look like the person I know. I go to the kitchen to take a break and get a glass of juice. I sit there and think of Calista as she was earlier in the week, when her face was messed up. That's not right, either. Finally I decide that I won't rely on pictures or memories. I will go deeper than that.

I will paint the real her.

FRIDAY

LAURA

"Laura, you're gonna be late!"

I'm standing in front of my bathroom mirror.

My mom is calling me down for breakfast.

I see a tiny pimple starting to form on my chin.

I close my eyes and then open them again.

Still there.

I lean in closer to the mirror.

"You gotta be kidding me," I say out loud, even though there's no one there. I'm talking to myself. It's come to that.

I rub my finger gently over the pimple, which is when I see two more, farther down, on my lower left cheek.

"I hate my life," I say to my mirror self, even though that's not true at all. Actually, I like my life a lot right now. I have nothing to complain about. I'm healthy. I do well in school. I'm a good athlete. I'm lucky, and I know it.

Still, these dang pimples.

My dad sticks his head in. "Hey, honey, let's go, you gotta eat something."

"It's fine, I'm just going to grab a quick bowl of cereal."

"Okay," he says, but he doesn't leave. "Whatcha doing?"

"Just washing up."

"Great." Still doesn't leave. "Dance tonight?"

"Yup."

"You're going to knock those boys dead, I'm telling ya."

"Okay, Dad." *Whatever you need to tell yourself.*

He finally leaves me alone, and I stare at my pimples for another minute. Then I go back to my room and pull my dress out of the closet. I hold it up and stare at it, then have this sudden intense desire to stomp on it, rip it into small pieces, and throw it in the trash. I hate it. It's ugly. I'm ugly. Even though I know I'm not. I'm kind of pretty, actually. I'm all of these things.

I'm complicated, okay? Who isn't?

My phone buzzes. A text.

HI, THIS IS DAMIAN.

Hmmmm, I think to myself. Then I type: HEY WHAT'S UP?

I put the dress back in the closet, then check the phone to see if he texted back. Nothing. I get dressed, brush my hair, brush my teeth, check the phone again. Still nothing. For some reason I start to get annoyed. I go downstairs. My mom is drinking coffee.

"Hi, my beautiful baby," she tells me.

"I don't love it when you call me that, actually," I tell her.

She stops, mid-sip. "Really?"

"Really."

"Okay, honey," she says. "I'm sorry."

"It's no big deal."

My phone buzzes.

DO YOU WANT TO MAYBE MEET UP AT THE DANCE?

I don't answer right away. I eat my cereal. After a minute, I look up at my mom. "I'm sorry, Mom. I didn't mean to snap at you. You can call me whatever you want."

My mom smiles. "How about if I just call you Laurabelle?" That's been her nickname for me since I was a baby.

"Laurabelle is great."

I text Damian back.

YEAH OKAY.

CALISTA

I'm standing in front of my bathroom mirror.

I can't see anything.

I mean, that's not true. I can see a lot. I just can't see anything except my face.

No pimple. No scar. No scab. No hives. No swelling. No dark circles under my eyes.

Nothing.

Just my face.

I look at it as if for the first time. Even though it's only been four days since the last time I saw it like this, it feels brand new.

I touch it, rub it, squeeze it. I make faces. I see if there's anything I can do to make it change. But I can't. My face is back and isn't going anywhere.

I feel whole.

There's a knock on the door. "Honey?"

I open it up, and my mom is standing there. She looks at my face and nods. "See? And you were so worried."

"I wasn't worried!"

"Okay, if you say so," she says. She peers into the mirror. "These things don't know everything, you know."

I frown. "What things?"

"Mirrors," she says. "They're just pieces of glass. They don't actually reflect anything about who we are. They're your friend one day, your enemy the next. You can't trust them!"

I laugh. "That's for sure."

She takes my face in her hands. "All I know is, you always look perfect to me, no matter what."

I lean against her shoulder.

That's what moms are for, I guess.

DAMIAN

I'm standing in front of my bathroom mirror, but I'm not looking at myself.

I'm looking down, at my phone.

HEY WHAT'S UP?

I stare at each word Laura wrote, trying to understand. HEY—hard to tell. WHAT'S UP—I can't decide. Is she being mean? Friendly? I hate texting. It's too confusing.

I type DO YOU WANT TO GO TO THE DANCE WITH ME? then immediately erase it. I type again. WOULD YOU HAVE ANY INTEREST IN GOING TO THE DANCE WITH ME? Erase.

I put my phone in my pocket and decide to try again later.

In the kitchen, my big sister, Janie, is stuffing books into her backpack. My mom has already left for work, as usual. Janie glances up. "Hey, you."

"Hey."

"I'm late, I gotta go," she says. "You all set? You got your shirts, your meds, blah blah blah?"

"I'm all set." I pour some milk into my raisin bran, spilling a little. I pick up my phone before it gets wet.

Janie messes up my hair, which I quickly put back in place.

"See you later," she says. "Big night, right?"

"I guess."

She laughs. "I remember middle school dances—they're a huge deal! Goofy, silly, ridiculous, and you'll laugh at it later, but it's huge. How's the poster coming?"

I point at a big portfolio case I left by the door. "Almost finished."

"Amazing. Can I see it?"

"Tonight, at the dance. When you pick me up."

"Whatever. As long as it's not another desert."

"It's not."

After she leaves, I eat my cereal and pick up my phone. I type: DO YOU WANT TO MAYBE MEET UP AT THE DANCE? Yeah, that's good enough. I hit send. I go to the closet to grab my jacket. I stare at it for a second, then put it on. I walk to the bus stop, holding the portfolio in one hand and my phone in the other. Finally, as the bus is pulling up, it buzzes. I pull it out and read the text.

YEAH OKAY.

I close my eyes and breathe.

CALISTA

The morning goes by in a blink. On my way into homeroom I run into Patrick, and his smile flashes at me just like it did five long days ago, when I thought he was the dreamiest boy in the world. My feelings about him are more complicated now, but his smile is still pretty impressive.

"Hey, Calista."

"Hey."

"Damian told me on the bus that he's almost finished with the poster."

"He'd better be—the dance is tonight!"

I can feel Ellie and Ella behind me, so I turn around.

"Calista!" Ellie gasps. "You have to sit with us at lunch today!"

"We have the most amazing news!" Ella titters.

I shrug. "Tell me now."

"We can't!" Ella looks around conspiratorially. "It's not for public consumption."

"Oooooh," Patrick says. "Sounds juicy."

"See you at lunch, okay?" Ellie says, a pleading look in her eyes.

"Sure, I guess." I watch them walk away, then turn back to Patrick. "Do you think they really have the most amazing news?"

"Of course not," he says. "But I do."

"Cut it out," I say.

I turn away before he sees me blush.

DAMIAN

In Spanish class, Laura sits all the way across the room from me. I see her looking at me once, and she half-smiles. I'm not sure what that means. All I know is I don't hear or understand anything the teacher says for the rest of the class, and it's not just because she's speaking a foreign language.

After class I walk out and there she is. "Damian, do you have a second?" she says.

"Oh, hey, I didn't see you there," I say, which is totally not true. "What's up?"

Laura gets right to the point. "Do you like Calista?"

I feel a line of sweat start to trickle down the bottom of my back.

"That's crazy. Where did you hear that?"

"Jeffrey is my friend Rachel's lab partner," she says. "He told her that he sits with you at lunch and you talk about Calista all the time."

I suddenly feel very mad at Jeffrey.

"That's crazy," I say. "As if a girl like Calista would be interested in me."

"That's not what I asked," Laura says, shaking her head. "I asked if you liked her."

I hesitate for a second before saying, "I don't know. Who doesn't?"

Then Laura does something shocking. She laughs. "Thank you for your honesty. So now let me ask you another question: Why would you want to go to the dance with me if you like Calista?"

"Because I like you, too," I say, before I can make something up.

"Good." Laura slips her backpack around her shoulders and starts to walk away. "Correct answer."

"So we're still going to the dance together, right?" I call out to her.

She gives me the thumbs-up without turning back.

I walk away, thinking one thing: it's a good thing I took an extra shirt to school after all.

LAURA

It turns out my dress is a little on the tight side, so I've made up my mind not to eat lunch today. That should solve everything.

Hey, a girl can dream, can't she?

I skip over the food line and head right to a table where Rachel is enjoying a full spread. Bless her heart, she just doesn't care. Or, maybe she cares, but it's not going to stop her from eating what she wants, when she wants. Or maybe she cares, and hates the way she looks, and eats to dull the pain. Any of those things are possible, but I don't know which, because we've never talked about it. There are some things you just don't talk about, even with your best friend.

"Where's your food?" Rachel asks me.

"Oh, uh, the line is too long," I say. "I'll go back in a little while."

"Okay." She takes a bite of something gloopy and

delicious-looking, then says, "Do you want to come over after practice?"

I'm confused. "Tonight?"

"Yeah!"

"Uh, the dance is tonight."

"I know, silly," Rachel says. "You can come over after practice and we can have dinner and play dress-up. We can do each other's hair and everything! Then we can go to the dance together."

I try to figure out the best way to say this. "Well, it turns out I might be meeting that guy Damian at the dance."

Rachel's eyes go wide. "Seriously? The artist kid with the red jacket?"

"Yeah," I say, suddenly feeling embarrassed by it. "You know, he asked me, and I couldn't say no, that kind of thing."

"Oh, got it," Rachel says. "Well, you can still come over before and we could still go together. If you want."

"Yeah, cool, maybe." That's all I say. I wish I'd gotten some lunch after all, so I could stall by taking a bite of whatever it was that I'd have. Because the truth is, I don't really want to go over to Rachel's house and get dressed. And the other truth is, I'm not sure I want to hang out with her at the dance. Because if we did, that means I'd kind of be responsible for her the whole time. And yeah, she's my best friend, and I'd do anything for her, as long as "anything" doesn't mean standing next to her making fun of the people who are dancing, as a way to make us feel better that we're not.

"What does 'maybe' mean?" Rachel asks.

"I think my mom really wants me to get dressed at home." It's the first thing that pops into my mind, and amazingly enough, it's actually the truth. "This is a big deal for her, my first formal dance and everything, and I think she might be sad if she didn't get to share it with me."

"Oh, right!" Rachel says. "That's so stupid of me not to realize that. I'm sorry for bringing it up."

"You don't have anything to be sorry for!" I take out my phone. "I'm going to send myself a note to text you right when I get there. I can't wait to see what you look like in that dress. You're going to look so gorgeous!"

"I know. I am, right?" Rachel says. "I'm going to rock it! We both are!" For the first time ever, I can sense a slightly desperate edge to her enthusiasm, but I pretend not to notice it, and to distract both her and myself, I help myself to a few of her fries.

They're delicious.

CALISTA

I come out of the lunch line and there it is.

My seat.

At my table.

Empty.

The same seat I sat in last year and thought I would sit in every day this year, right up until a few days ago.

Ella and Ellie are waving me over. They're back in their usual seats, too, as is everyone else.

It's like nothing has changed. Except a lot has.

"Welcome back," says Camille, from her side of the table. "What was it like out there in the real world?"

"Hahaha, very funny," says Ella, shutting Camille down.

Ellie grabs my arm. "Come on, we have a lot to talk about."

Before I sit, I glance around the cafeteria, and my eyes

land on the table where I sat on Wednesday, with Beth, Kara and Shelby. I wave to them and shrug. They wave back and laugh.

"Who's that?" asks Ellie, pulling me down into my seat.

"Friends," I say.

"Seriously?"

"Yes, seriously. Some girls I met the other day. They're pretty awesome."

Ellie looks wounded. "Well then, why don't you just sit with them then?"

I roll my eyes. "What was it you wanted to tell me? You said it was really important."

"Oh, right!" Ellie glances at Ella. "Do you want to tell her, or should I?"

"You tell her," Ella says.

"Okay, fine." Ellie leans in like she's about to give me a secret code to the country's nuclear weapons. "We fixed things between you and Patrick."

"What are you talking about? Fixed what things?"

"Tonight. The dance. It's all set."

I glance over at Patrick, who's at his usual table. He smiles. Will, who is sitting right next to him, gives me two thumbs-up and hollers, "Let's do this!" Patrick smacks Will in the back of the head.

"I don't understand," I say to Ellie and Ella. "What's all set?"

"He wants to take you after all," Ella says. "He told Ellie this morning. She was upset at first but then she totally got it."

"We told him you'd love to," Ellie says. "You and him were meant to be together. It's fine, and besides, I'm going to go with Will, so we can all hang out together if we want!"

I stare at them in disbelief. "You said yes? For me? Without even asking me?"

"Well, yeah, duh," Ellie says. "We talked about this, remember? On Monday?"

"Yeah, that was then. This is now."

"I'm sorry," Ella says. "Did we do something wrong?"

"A couple of days ago I heard you call me a witch," I say to Ellie. "And how it made total sense that Patrick wouldn't want to take me to the dance."

"I never said that," Ellie says, a hint of panic in her voice.

"Yes, you did."

"Well, if I said it, it was just because you were being mean."

"Being mean? I'd just had my nose practically broken!"

Ellie looks like I just punched *her* in the nose.

I say the next thing that pops into my head, which surprises everyone, including me. "And anyway, I can't go with Patrick."

In the silence that follows, I hear Camille whisper, "This is getting good."

"Why not?!" shrieks Ellie.

I stand up. "I'm going with someone else."

And I start walking away.

DAMIAN

It feels like a scene in a movie I've seen before.

Calista is back in her usual seat. She's looking over at Patrick. Patrick is smiling at her. Will is acting like an idiot.

"Stop staring," Jeffrey says. Today he's eating a tuna fish and onion sandwich. As if he doesn't have enough trouble making friends.

"I'm not staring," I say. "It's happening right in front of me. What am I supposed to do, turn away?"

"Yes," Jeffrey says. "Laura is looking at you."

I feel my ears turn red. "She is?"

"Yes."

I glance over to Laura's table. Sure enough, she's watching me watch Calista.

I stand up to walk over to Laura's table, which is when I see Calista stand up and start walking toward me.

A blast of moisture explodes underneath my arms.

LAURA

"Callie?" I call, as she goes by me, but she doesn't slow down.

I get up and follow.

"Don't," I hear Rachel say.

I pretend not to hear her.

CALISTA

I get to Damian's table, but this time, I stay far away from his elbows.

"Your face looks a lot better," says his friend, whose name I think is Jesse.

"Thanks," I say. An odd smell crosses my nose. "What kind of sandwich is that?"

Damian's friend doesn't answer me. Instead, he just stuffs the rest of whatever it is into his mouth.

I look at Damian. "So, uh, can I see the poster?"

"I'm actually not quite done with it," he tells me. "I'm finishing it up after school."

"I thought Patrick said you were done."

"Almost."

"Okay."

After a few seconds, I add, "You can ask me to the dance if you want."

He blinks ten times in two seconds. "What?"

"You can ask me to the dance," I repeat. "I'll go with you."

"Why? What happened?"

"My friends are annoying me, that's what happened," I say, feeling stressed out. "So, do you want to go with me or not?"

"I—uh—"

"See you tonight?" I say, trying not to get impatient.

"Uh—oh, yeah—okay," stammers Damian.

I turn around to go back to my table, and bump right into Laura.

LAURA

All I hear is, "See you tonight?" and "Uh, yeah, okay." But what I see convinces me it's not as simple as that.

"What are you guys talking about?" I ask.

"Nothing," says Damian.

"Damian and I are just going to meet up later at the dance," Calista says, and starts to walk away.

I feel my heart jump to a higher rate.

"Hold on a second," Damian says, like a scared little boy.

Calista turns back. "What?"

We both look at Damian, who has suddenly been stripped of the ability to speak.

"He asked me to go to the dance with him this morning," I tell Calista.

"No way!" blurts out Jeffrey. "Cool!" I can smell his onion breath from where I'm standing, and that's not a compliment.

I try to sound completely calm. "Damian, if you'd rather go with Calista, you could have just told me."

"Calista asked me!" Damian says, but he can't look at me. "I didn't ask her."

"Wait a second, Laura, hold on," Calista says. "You told me you had no interest in Damian!"

Damian starts biting his nails. "You did?"

I realize I've lost any moral advantage I might have had, but instead of making me embarrassed, it only makes me mad. "That was yesterday!" I snap at Damian. "Callie was pressuring me to go to the dance with you! It was—it was like we were both charity cases, or something."

Damian stares at me, then at Calista. "Really? Charity cases?"

"Of course not!" Calista throws her hands up in the air. "I was just trying to be nice! Fine, forget it, forget the whole thing! Maybe I'll go with Patrick after all! Gorgeous, nice, UNSWEATY PATRICK!"

"Fine!" I say. "And I'll go with myself!"

We both stomp away in opposite directions, with Calista knocking over Jeffrey's chocolate milk in the process. "Sorry, Jesse," she says, without looking back.

"It's Jeffrey," Jeffrey says, but no one is listening to him.

CALISTA

I get back to my table, grab my tray, and walk over to Beth's table. "Can I sit with you guys?"

"Of course," she says. Shelby and Kara quickly slide over, making room for me.

I sit and start eating. I can feel them all looking at me for a few seconds, then they go back to their conversation. I barely know these girls, but they know enough to do exactly the right thing.

Sometimes the nicest thing people can do is to leave you alone.

LAURA

As I head back to my seat, I pass Ellie and Ella's table, and I overhear Ellie say to Ella, "What is with Calista? She got so weird when she was ugly."

DAMIAN

"Wow," Jeffrey says. "That was intense."

I don't answer. Instead, I take a few more bites of my sandwich and then get up, discard my tray, walk down to the art room, pull out the poster, and put it on the easel.

Then I finally finish the painting.

LAURA

I'm one of the first ones at soccer practice, as usual. I start putting my cleats on when I hear Coach Sweeney let out a little whistle. "Huh," she says.

I glance up to see Calista walking toward us. She's dressed and ready to go.

I'm shocked, but not surprised.

"Well," says Coach. "Look what the cat dragged in. And on time, for once."

"Hey, Coach," says Calista. "I'm really sorry I missed the last few days."

"I heard all about it," says Coach. "You feeling okay?"

"Yup." Calista reaches into her bag and pulls out something that looks like the mask from *The Phantom of the Opera*. She straps it around her face.

"Nice touch, Callie," I say, without looking at her.

"Thanks," Calista says, without looking at me.

Neither one of us mentions what happened at lunch.

But I'm thinking about it, and I'm pretty sure she is, too.

The rest of the girls start arriving, all doing a double take when they see Calista and her facial contraption. Most people give her an awkward smile and say something like "Glad you're here" or "Welcome back," but Rachel gives her a big hug. Calista looks stunned, and then grateful.

"I can't believe it! I thought you quit!" Rachel says to Calista during stretching, loud enough for everyone to hear.

"Well, turns out I didn't," Calista says. Then she glances at me and says, "Sometimes I say things I don't mean."

"Ain't that the truth," I say, returning the glance.

"What happened to those friends of yours, Effie and Emma?" Rachel exclaims. "They're going to be so mad!"

"Effie and Emma?" Calista says.

"You mean Evelyn and Edna," I say.

Suddenly Calista and I both burst out laughing—and just like that, the tension eases a little bit.

"I was just upset a few days ago," Calista says to Rachel. "It had nothing to do with you guys or the team or anything. I was just confused. But I want to play soccer and I'm here."

"Sweet!" Rachel says. "You better score a lot of goals for us this year, okay?"

"I'll try," Calista says.

Coach blows her whistle. "Three-on-two shooting drill! Let's go!"

Practice is intense. As usual, I'm matched up against Calista during the scrimmage. She's running me ragged. The girl can really play. She gets off a few good shots, but Rachel saves them all, until the last minute, when Calista fakes me out of my shoes, goes around me and puts one into the upper left corner. Rachel can only watch as the ball rockets past her.

"Dang," Rachel says. "That was nasty."

Coach Sweeney's whistle screams. "That's it!" she hollers. "Bring it in!"

As we all head to the sideline, Calista takes her mask off. Her face is dripping.

"You're sweating like a pig," I tell her.

"I know," she says. "I actually love to sweat. It feels good."

"Not to Damian it doesn't," I say.

Calista stops walking and stares at me.

"Dang it," she says, and I know just how she feels.

DAMIAN

I realize as I walk into the school that I've never been there at night before.

None of the concerts; none of the dances; not even the art exhibit at the end of last year, even though Mrs. Henshaw begged me to come. My drawings were there, but I wasn't. I wasn't ready.

The lights are bright as Janie pulls into the parking lot. I put my jacket on.

"Have fun, dude," she says. "Text me when you need me to pick you up."

"I will," I tell her. "Be ready."

She laughs. "Stop it. Come on, have fun. You can do it, I know you can!"

"I'll try," I say.

I get out of the car, staring down at my phone. Laura and Calista both texted me earlier, while I was home eating dinner. CAN WE TALK? Laura's said. Calista's said I'M REALLY SORRY!

I didn't answer either one.

I walk into the cafeteria and see the decorations and punch bowls and snacks all set up. I ignore the urge to run away.

"Hey, Damian!" I look up and see Nurse Kline walking over to me. "It's so good to see you!"

"Hey, Nurse Kline. It's good to see you, too."

She smacks me on the arm. "It is not! Don't you lie to me, Damian White. We've been through far too much together."

"I'm not lying," I say. "It's always good to see you."

"Awww." She gives me a little hug. "Well, I hope you dance your little heart out tonight. Hey, I want to see your poster! Where is it?"

"I'm going down to the art room to get it right now, actually," I tell her.

"Can't wait!" She gives me a wave as I head down the hall, past the parent volunteers spying on their kids, past the custodians pushing tables up against the wall, past the A/V Club setting up the sound system, past the boys who are laughing and pushing each other against lockers, past the girls who are giggling and running in and out of the bathroom, past the teachers who are mad about having to work at night, and around the corner to where the art studio is. It will be good to be alone for a few minutes, to collect my thoughts and get myself ready for the night ahead.

Only, I'm not alone.

I walk in and see Calista, Laura, and Patrick. They look up and see me. Again, I resist the urge to run away.

It's harder this time.

CALISTA

After helping move the tables and chairs to the side of the cafeteria, I head down to the art studio, where Laura and I had agreed to meet and wait for Damian.

Patrick wasn't part of the plan, but when I walk in, there he is, standing with Laura.

She looks up and smiles. He looks up and tries to smile.

"Hey," I say. "What are you doing here?"

"I wanted to finally see the darn painting," he says. A few seconds later, he adds, "Uh, Calista? I didn't mean to cause all that stuff between you and Ellie and Ella. I really didn't."

"It's okay," I tell him. "I'm kind of glad it happened, to tell you the truth."

"Really?" he asks. "Why?"

"Because sometimes you need crazy stuff to happen, so you can remember who your real friends are."

I throw a look to Laura, and she catches it. It's a perfect catch.

There's a noise at the door, and we all look up to see Damian standing there. He sees us and freezes. I can see the sweat forming on his forehead. "What are you guys doing here?" he asks.

For some reason, the first thing that pops into my head is that he's wearing his red jacket. I thought maybe he'd leave it at home this time.

"Hey, Rembrandt," Patrick says. "I don't know what these lovely ladies are doing here, but can I see this great work of art already?"

"I . . . Uh . . . I can't."

"You can't? What, it's still not ready?" Patrick stands up. "You've been working on this thing for three days!"

"Patrick, stop it," I say. "Damian will show it to us when he's ready."

"Fine." He throws up his hands and sits down in a chair.

Laura walks over to Damian, who is still standing in the doorway. "Calista and I came here to apologize."

"I acted like a jerk," I chime in. "At lunch. What I said . . . I'm really sorry."

"Nobody meant to make you feel bad," Laura says. "Especially me."

"Okay," says Damian, still not looking at either Laura

or myself. "So, is it okay if I ask gorgeous, nice, unsweaty Patrick for a favor?"

Laura and I laugh, but Patrick doesn't get it. "Yeah, sure. What's up?" he asks.

"Can you help me carry the poster into the cafeteria?" Damian asks him.

Patrick blinks in confusion. "I thought you said it wasn't ready?"

"I didn't say that, you said that," Damian says. "I just said you couldn't see it. Of course it's ready. The dance starts in five minutes."

"Oh, yeah," Patrick says. "Right."

Damian walks over to Mrs. Henshaw's office and takes out the poster, which is wrapped in giant brown paper. "Mrs. Henshaw says it's tradition to reveal the painting in front of the whole school, right at the beginning of the dance. She says it's more dramatic that way."

Patrick rolls his eyes. "Whatever." He picks up one side of the poster and Damian grabs the other. They start to walk out.

I call out to him. "Damian?"

He stops and looks at me. "Yeah?"

"You're nobody's charity case," I say. "You're a really nice person and a very talented artist."

He finally cracks a small smile. "I appreciate that, thank you."

"Let's go," Laura says. "The suspense is killing me."

"It's just a poster," Damian says. "It's not, like, life or death or anything."

Patrick laughs. "Tell that to Calista! She's freaking out right now."

"Quiet!" I bark at Patrick.

He's right, of course.

LAURA

As the four of us walk down the hall, a strange feeling comes over me. At first, I can't tell what it is, but then I get it. It's the feeling of superiority. I'm walking with Calista and Patrick, the two best-looking, most popular people in our grade. I can't help it; it makes me feel cool. Everyone is looking at us. Wishing they were us. Wishing they were me. In this moment, I know what being as popular as Calista and Patrick feels like.

It's an illusion, of course, but I'll take it.

As soon as we get to the cafeteria, the overhead lights start to dim. Everyone screams in anticipation. Someone spills soda on me. I turn around but they're gone. Somehow, the floor is already sticky.

I glance across the dance floor and see Rachel with Danielle and Becky, two other girls from the soccer team. They're cracking up at something. I wave, but Rachel doesn't see me. Or maybe she pretends not to see me. I can't be sure which.

"May I have everyone's attention, please?"

A spotlight goes up on the little stage in the front of the cafeteria. Dr. Michener is standing there, with a microphone in her hand. Next to her is Mrs. Henshaw, the art teacher.

"Thank you all so much for coming tonight. We are so happy to begin another school year here at Silver Lane Middle School, and what better way to kick things off than with the First Week Dance."

Another huge scream and cheer. Dr. Michener waits patiently for it to die down.

"This is the ninth year of this fabulous annual tradition. And as we do every year, we've asked an eighth-grade artist to draw the poster for this year's dance. The poster will remain on display in the office throughout the first quarter of the year, and then be mounted next to all the other First Week Dance posters in the hallway leading to the Main Office." Dr. Michener turns around. "And now, I'd like to ask Mrs. Henshaw to invite the artist and our two models up to the stage."

Everyone cheers as Damian, Calista, and Patrick step forward. All of a sudden, I'm standing by myself. Even though most of the lights are off, I still feel totally exposed. It seems like everyone is staring at me, but of course they're not.

"Thank you, Dr. Michener," says Mrs. Henshaw. "I'm very pleased to say that we've chosen an extraordinary artist to create the poster for this year. He is a wonderfully talented, outstanding young man. Please give a warm hand for Damian White."

More applause as Damian puts his hand up and waves shyly.

"As for our student models this year," continues Mrs. Henshaw, "we couldn't have asked for two more ideal candidates. Both Calista Getz and Patrick Toole are very good sports for agreeing to pose after school this week. And Calista is even a dance student, so she was able to coach Patrick along!" They both smile and giggle as laughter ripples through the crowd. Calista is twirling her hair just behind her left ear, which means she's nervous.

"So," Mrs. Henshaw says. "The moment we've been waiting for. Damian, please do the honors and unveil the poster for this year's First Week Dance!"

I can feel the anticipation in the crowd as Damian walks up to the giant poster. He pauses for just one second, and he wipes his forehead with the sleeve of his red jacket. Then he takes a deep breath, and in one quick motion rips the brown paper off the frame, revealing the poster underneath.

I lean in closer to examine it. Everyone does.

At first I can't quite tell what's happening in the painting, then it slowly comes into focus.

Two figures are intertwined with the night sky, dancing through the solar system. Patrick looks amazing, almost like a god, as he is seen spinning a female figure through space.

The female figure, however, isn't Calista.

Or is it?

I step forward, just as everyone starts to murmur. As I get closer, I see why they're murmuring. The body looks like Calista. The hair looks like Calista. But the face is something completely bizarre and unrecognizable. It's contorted and misshapen, almost like a gargoyle, or some sort of ogre. The eyes are in the wrong place and the nose has only one nostril. The skin is red on the left side of the face, and blue on the right. The only part that looks like Calista is the mouth and the smile. It is definitely her smile.

The face is bizarre, and freaky, and stunning, and brave, and terrible, and beautiful.

It takes a minute for the room to realize what is happening. Murmurings start to rumble through the crowd. "Is that Calista?" "What happened to her?" "The poor thing."

Then, the laughter starts.

At first, only a few kids are giggling, but then, slowly, it starts to ripple throughout the room.

Soon, the only thing you can hear is roaring laughter. The whole student body, laughing at Calista. Or, some freaky version of her.

"It's not funny!" I say, but no one can hear me. "It's not funny!" I scream, louder.

My eyes search for Calista, but I can't see her—too many people are crowding around the painting. Then, suddenly, there she is. She's off the stage. Her head is in her hands. Dr. Michener is trying to comfort her.

I'm not sure what to do. I glance back at the painting and notice something I hadn't seen before.

Damian has painted gold lettering just above the figures.

THIS YEAR, LET'S REACH FOR THE STARS.

CALISTA

At first, I have no idea what I'm looking at.

That's not me.

That can't be me.

The room is silent. Everyone is staring at the painting, except for one person. Damian.

He is staring at me, waiting for my reaction. I can feel his eyes on me, even though I can't look at him. I can't look at anyone except myself.

Or I should say, that horrible version of myself.

I feel my eyes start to well up, and finally I turn away. I can hear people whispering, wondering, asking each other, "Is that her?"

I hear a voice I recognize. "Oh my GOD!"

Ellie, of course.

She is shrieking with laughter. "That is AMAZING!"

Ella's voice comes next. "No WAY! No WAY!"

I can't help myself. I look over at them, but they don't

see me, because they're staring into their phones, taking pictures of the poster, no doubt getting ready to post them online for others to enjoy. More and more people take out their phones to do the same thing.

Then I hear a noise. It gets louder. People are laughing. Laughing at me.

"Are you okay? Calista?" I look up to see Dr. Michener standing over me, and I realize I must have sat down at some point. I'm sitting on the edge of the stage, but she reaches down to pull me up, and I let her. She steers me off to the side, out of the light, where finally I let the tears come.

"Why would he do this to me?" I stammer.

Dr. Michener shakes her head. "I'm not quite sure. But it's important to remember, artists interpret real life for their own vision. That's what they do. Picasso, perhaps the greatest artist of them all, painted some of the most beautiful women in the world, and made them look very unusual. But their beauty was still very much alive."

"Calista," a voice says. Patrick is standing there, unsure of what to do, where to go. "Are you okay? I'm really sorry about this."

"Go away, please," I say, and before either of us can say anything else Will pounces on his back. "Awesome poster!" Will bellows. "You guys look like the perfect couple up there in space! Just don't scare all the planets! HAHAHAHAHA!"

Patrick says something, but I'm too far away to hear it. I don't even realize it, but I'm on the move. I'm walking, then running.

"Calista?" calls the principal. "Are you all right? Where are you going?"

That's a good question, I say to myself.

If only I knew the answer.

DAMIAN

I see Calista talking to Dr. Michener. I want to do something, say something, but I can't because Mrs. Henshaw is talking to me.

". . . not in the spirit of the assignment," she is saying. I missed the first part of the sentence, but I'm pretty sure I get the gist of what she's saying.

"I'm sorry," I say to her. "I'm sorry."

"I just don't understand." Mrs. Henshaw shakes her head. "You're a very interesting artist, Damian, and all artists should have original ideas of course, but this is taking it too far. What were you thinking?"

"I don't know," I say. "It just happened."

"Well, I'm quite sure we cannot hang this poster in the hall."

"Okay," I say. "Will you excuse me? I have to go."

"What? Go where?" says Mrs. Henshaw, but I don't answer her. I see Calista walking, then running out of the cafeteria. I start to follow her but feel a hand on my shoulder. I turn to see Jeffrey standing there, eyes wide.

"Dude!" he says, over and over again. "Dude! Dude! That drawing is like, super intense!"

"I have to go," I say to him. "And it's a painting, not a drawing."

"You're like, a true artist!" Jeffrey yells.

I ignore him and start running again, hoping no one else will stop me.

But someone does.

CALISTA

I wind up in the gym.

For some reason, the lights are on. Then I remember that they always keep the gym open for dances, so the kids who are too shy to actually dance can hang out in here, shooting baskets. I've never been one of those kids before. But I'm one now.

I take off my high heels and start shooting baskets.

Swish. Swish. Swish. I sink six in a row before I finally clank one off the rim. It must be the ball's fault. I kick it to the other side of the gym.

I feel like a character in one of those movies where someone who's about to die sees their whole life flash before their eyes. But I'm not dying—except on the inside—and it's not my whole life that flashes before my eyes, just the last week. The pimple. The rash. The bashed nose and the black eyes. The mall. The book. The nurse's office. The fights with Ellie and Ella. The fights with Laura.

The trip from pretty to ugly and back, and then back again to uglier than ever. The confusion about who my friends really are—about *what* friends really are. I thought Damian had become my friend.

I guess I was wrong.

I run down to the other side of the gym and start shooting on the other basket. Four more swishes in a row. I'm really on fire tonight, for some strange reason.

The gym door opens.

I whirl around, expecting to tell whomever it is to go away. I'm not in the mood for anyone trying to make me feel better. I just want to be alone.

It's Mr. Cody, my English teacher.

Not who I was expecting.

I don't say anything, and neither does he. In fact, he just stands there, at the door of the gym. Not moving. After a minute, I start shooting again. The shots aren't falling anymore. That's what happens sometimes—hot one minute, cold the next.

I shoot, the ball clanks off the rim and into Mr. Cody's hands. I'm not even sure how he got under the basket, but there he is. He passes the ball back to me, still not saying anything.

I shoot ten more times, he gets ten more rebounds.

"What?" I say finally.

"What, what?" he says back.

"What do you want?"

"To rebound your shots."

Seven more shots. Five misses.

"Remember in *Curious Incident*," Mr. Cody says after the seventh shot, "when Christopher goes by himself to London to find his mom?"

I hold the ball. "Yeah, why?"

Mr. Cody shrugs. "I liked that part."

"It was okay."

"What was your favorite part?"

"I guess the ending."

He nods. "You mean the ending that you pretended you'd already read, the first time I asked you about it? That ending?"

I refuse to smile. "Yep, that's the one."

After I make the next shot, Mr. Cody holds the ball. "Damian is waiting by the door. Can I tell him he can come in and talk to you?"

"No."

"He really wants to talk to you."

"No."

Six more shots. Five misses.

"Fine," I say.

I see Mr. Cody look toward the door and nod. I keep shooting until I hear Damian's voice. "Hey."

"I'm going to go see how the dance is going," Mr. Cody says. "I'm also going to lock the door, so no one else can come in. When you guys are done in here, just leave it open."

"Okay," I say.

"See ya," he says.

I take three more shots. Swish. Swish. Swish.

Looks like I'm hot again.

DAMIAN

Calista keeps shooting. She doesn't look at me. I don't blame her.

Finally, I decide what to say.

"I thought you would like it," I say.

She doesn't answer. Just takes more shots. Most of them go in.

"I didn't realize you were so good at basketball," I say.

"You didn't realize a lot of things," she says.

I don't have an answer for that, so instead I say, "Want to play one-on-one?"

She looks at me, finally. "Seriously? Absolutely not."

"Okay."

After another minute, I ask again. "Are you sure?"

She laughs, sadly. "You're crazy."

"I guess."

"Okay," she says. "One game."

We start playing. I take it easy at first, and she goes

ahead, 2-0. Finally I decide to use my height advantage and score three quick baskets. I take an outside shot—nothing but net.

"Nice shot," she says. We're both starting to breathe hard.

"Thanks."

She points at my jacket. "Are you going to wear that for the rest of your life?"

"I don't know," I say. "Maybe."

The score is tied 6-6 when she makes a nice drive to the basket. I could easily block her shot but I decide not to. It goes in.

"Game," I say.

"You gotta win by two," she says, and immediately hits a three-pointer. "Now it's game. Even though you let me win." She heaves the ball down to the other end of the court. "It's the least you could do, I guess."

"I thought you would like the poster," I say, again. "I really did."

"YOU THOUGHT I WOULD LIKE IT?" She's yelling now, all of a sudden.

"Yes, for some reason I did," I say. "I guess—I guess I thought you would get it."

"Get what?" she says, a little calmer, but not much. "That you think I'm ugly? That I'm disgusting? That I'm GROSS??!?"

"NO!" I say, raising my own voice.

We're both breathing really hard now, and it's not just from basketball. I can feel the sweat dripping down the front of my neck.

"I just don't—I want to go home," Calista says, and she starts to leave.

"You're a lot of different things!" I blurt out.

She stops. "Excuse me?"

I pause for a second. "I thought you would get that I was painting you as a lot of different things, with a lot of different feelings. Because that's who you are." I walk up to her. "You're nice, but sometimes you can be mean. You're like the most popular girl in school, but some-times you can be lonely and insecure. And sometimes you think you're ugly, even though you're beautiful."

"That's the craziest thing I ever heard," she says, but her eyes are a little softer. "And thanks for making me ten times more insecure than I ever was before, by the way," she adds.

I take off my jacket, and wipe my face with my shirt sleeves. "I didn't mean to do that."

"Well, what about Patrick?" she asks, sitting down in the bleachers. "Why did you paint him like the most handsome kid ever?"

"Because I don't know anything about who Patrick is. All I know is what he looks like." I sit down near her, but not right next to her. "I know a lot more about you. I feel like . . . I feel like I know the real you."

Calista turns to look at me. "You should have told me what you were doing."

"I was too nervous."

"For good reason."

"I'm really sorry," I say.

We sit there and don't say anything for about five minutes. Suddenly she stands up. "Okay. Let's go back."

I feel myself blinking. "Seriously?"

"Yes, seriously," she says. "Now hurry up, before I change my mind."

We prop the door open, and we're halfway down the hall toward the cafeteria when Calista stops me. "Your jacket. You left it on the bleachers."

I hesitate, and my heart skip a few beats. Then I keep walking.

"It's okay," I say. "Leave it."

CALISTA

Damian and I walk back to the cafeteria. His shirt is soaked through, but he doesn't seem to care. Maybe because I'm sweating, too.

A bunch of people see us coming and come flying toward us. Ellie and Ella barge their way to the front.

"Calista!" says Ellie. "What's going on? Are you upset?"

"Do you want me to be?" I ask her.

Ellie pouts. "Of course not!"

"Can we be best friends again?" Ella asks. "You look gorgeous tonight, by the way."

"Do you guys know Damian?" I ask. "He's a friend of mine."

Ellie looks shocked as her eyes dart from Damian to me. "Seriously? He just painted you to look like a total ugly hag."

"Yeah, but a complicated ugly hag with a lot of interesting feelings," I say.

"Oh," says Ellie, thoroughly confused.

"Excuse me," Damian says. "Do either of you two want to pose for my next painting?"

"Um," says Ella, before Ellie interrupts her with, "Yeah, uh, we're gonna go get some punch. Calista, find us later? You look so amazing. Did I say that already?"

"Yup, you did," I say. "So do you."

After they walk away, Damian and I look at each other and smile and shake our heads.

"I need you to do me a favor," I tell Damian. "Can you get something for me?"

He cocks his head. "Depends on what it is."

I tell him, but I don't think he believes me.

LAURA

The music is playing, but no one is really dancing or doing much of anything. Everyone seems to be waiting. I don't blame them. I'm waiting, too.

Finally I see Calista and Damian coming down the hall, heading toward the cafeteria. I start walking over, but Ellie and Ella get to them first. Of course they do. I stop in my tracks.

"Waiting your turn?" Rachel asks. I didn't even realize she was standing there.

"I just want to make sure she's okay," I say.

"That's nice."

I turn to look at Rachel. "I'm sorry I didn't come to the dance with you tonight. The whole thing was a big misunderstanding."

She takes a sip of her punch. "I guess life is a big misunderstanding, isn't it? That's what makes it interesting."

"Ha! I guess so." I turn to her. "That dress is gorgeous, by the way."

"Thanks," she says, laughing. "Better the dress than nothing."

"Stop it, you look gorgeous, too."

"So do you."

"Yay us!" I say, and we hug.

For the moment, that's good enough.

I glance up and see Ellie and Ella walk away, then Calista whisper something to Damian. He walks away, too, which leaves Calista standing there alone.

"Can you excuse me for a minute?" I ask Rachel. She nods, and I walk quickly over to Calista. She sees me coming, and I expect her to look stressed. But instead, she gives me a little smile.

"Laurasaurus," she says.

"Hey, Callie." We hug. It's the thing to do tonight, I guess. "Are you okay?"

She nods. "I'm okay." She smiles, a bit shyly. "I guess I kind of made a mess of things."

"We made a mess of things," I correct her. "It was a crazy week. Things happen."

"They sure do." Calista is staring up at the poster. I follow her eyes and stare at it, too. "What do you think?" she asks.

"I think it's a work of art," I tell her.

Damian returns. "Here you go." He hands her a magic marker.

"It is a work of art," Calista says. "But it's not quite finished."

And she walks up onto the stage.

CALISTA

I walk up to Dr. Michener and tell her what I want to do. She tells me it's okay. Then I nod at Damian, and he tells the A/V kids to cut the music. The lights get turned on and everyone falls silent. All eyes turn to me as I pick up the microphone.

"Hey, everyone," I say. My heart is racing a hundred miles an hour and I can feel the blood pumping in my ears. But I manage to plow ahead.

"I have always been judged by how I look," I say. "And I'm a really lucky person. I totally get that." I see Laura in the crowd and I smile at her. She smiles back.

"But the funny thing is, when people think you're pretty, they also think other things. Like, you shouldn't play sports. Or, you can't be smart. Or, you shouldn't have friends that might be different from you."

"You mean ugly!" someone yells, and everyone laughs.

"No, I DON'T mean ugly," I say, raising my voice. "I mean different."

The room is quiet again.

"This week, I learned a lot about myself. It was hard. But it was good." I walk over to the poster. "Damian White is an incredible artist and this poster is beautiful. But it doesn't quite show who I really am."

"That's for sure!" That one was Will Hanson, I can tell. This time, I laugh along with everyone else. Then I take out the magic marker, and I draw a giant black dot right in the middle of my single-nostril nose.

"There," I say. "Now it's the real me. Pimples and all."

I put the microphone back in the stand, hand the magic marker to Mrs. Henshaw, and jump off the stage. People are still quiet. No one is sure quite what to do. I hear a couple of people clapping, and I see that it's Laura and Rachel.

"You guys rock," I tell them.

I feel a hand on my shoulder, and it's Patrick. He looks so handsome in his suit, and his perfect haircut, and his blinding smile.

"I was wondering," he says, "if you would dance with me?"

"Of course I will, just not yet, okay?" I say. "I'll find you later." Then I turn and look around until I see Damian, who's talking to his friend from the lunch table. I walk over to them.

"Hey, Damian," I say. "Hey, Jeffrey."

Damian elbows Jeffrey in the ribs. "She remembered your name."

"Cut it out," Jeffrey says, but I have to admit—he looks pretty excited.

I look at Damian. "Will you come with me for a second?"

"To where?"

"Not far."

I take his hand and we walk over to Laura and Rachel.

"Can I borrow your friend for a second?" I ask Rachel.

"Sure," she says.

"Wherever we're going, I want Rachel to come, too," Laura says. "I'm here with her."

Rachel's eyes are shining, but she shakes her head. "You go ahead," she says to Laura.

Laura puts her head on Rachel's shoulder for a second, then nods at me. "Okay."

I pull Damian and Laura out to the middle of the cafeteria, where the dancing is supposed to happen. The dance floor is empty, though, for obvious reasons.

Damian's hands are a little wet.

"Are you doing what I think you're doing?" Laura asks.

I nod. "I think we should dance."

Laura laughs. "You're serious? There's no music playing."

"I couldn't be serious-er," I tell her.

"I've never danced in public before," Laura says.

"I've never been to a dance before," Damian says.

"Well," I say, "I've never gotten a pimple before. I guess there's a first time for everything, huh?"

We all laugh and decide to go for it. Laura turns out to be a much better dancer than me. Sadly, I can't say the same about Damian.

"This is painful," he moans.

"Just relax, and be yourself," I tell him. "If I can be the real me, then you can be the real you."

Damian raises his eyebrows. "So we're the real us?"

"Yup, that's who we are," Laura says. "The real us."

We all laugh and start jumping around like crazy people. After a few seconds, the lights suddenly go down, and the music gets cranked up.

Soon, the dance floor is full.

Acknowledgments

Books are always an us, never a me. Thanks to Lauren Burniac for shepherding this book from afar, and the incredible team at Roaring Brook for shepherding it from anear.